I0456833

A STEP BACK
IN TIME

DEBBIE CHASE

This is a work of fiction. Names, characters, places, and incidents are products of the author's imagination or are used fictitiously and are not to be construed as real. Any resemblance to actual events, locations, organizations, or persons, living or dead, is entirely coincidental.

World Castle Publishing, LLC
Pensacola, Florida
Copyright © Debbie Chase 2019
Paperback ISBN: 9781950890040
eBook ISBN: 9781950890057
First Edition World Castle Publishing, LLC, May 27, 2019
http://www.worldcastlepublishing.com
Licensing Notes
All rights reserved. No part of this book may be used or reproduced in any manner whatsoever without written permission, except in the case of brief quotations embodied in articles and reviews.
Cover: Karen Fuller
Editor: Maxine Bringenberg

Chapter One

"Hannah...hey.... Hannah...wake up...."

Groggily I opened my eyes, the room swimming around me. What was going on? One minute I was busily typing up a very complicated will (where somebody was leaving far too much money to their beloved pet dog), and then...well, I wasn't sure. A hazy memory of a woman wearing a long black gown came to mind, and then nothing...blank....

"Hannah?" Max Reynolds, his expression concerned (for once), appeared in my vision. He stared at me intently, his green eyes narrowed, a lock of blond hair falling onto his forehead which, impatiently, he pushed away with his fingers.

"Oh hi," I said, my voice just a tiny whisper. What was wrong with me? Had I been drugged? Surely not. Who could have done it anyway? Max? I eyed him warily.

"Falling asleep on the job?" he asked. "Do you realize how serious that is? A sacking offense." He laughed loudly at his own wit. Oh, so typical of Max. "Methinks maybe you need a good old shot of caffeine."

"Yeah, maybe you're right—I'll make some coffee." As if from a long, long way away noises started to come back; the ringing of phones, Sarah clicking away at her computer in the office next door, the murmur of voices from upstairs.

My legs wobbling slightly, I stood up and began to make my way to the little kitchen that adjoined the office.

"Oh, Hannah, while you're there, make me a cup, will you? You know how I like it—milk, no sugar?" Inwardly fuming, I watched Max's retreating back, the laddish swagger in his walk. He grinned cheekily over his shoulder and said, "I'll be in my office."

"Who does he think he is?" I asked myself as I thumped on the kettle and began taking mugs from the cupboard, milk from the fridge. While waiting for the kettle to boil I gazed from the tiny mullioned window at the paved courtyard at the back of the offices. Well, it was offices now, but had once apparently been a row of cottages, as had the pub next door, and still held a lot of old-fashioned charm. There were beautiful tiled fireplaces in every room, even in the offices upstairs that would once have been bedrooms, and thick black beams crisscrossed the ceilings. It pleased me to think that the office I worked in would once have been a dining room.

It was April, and bright yellow daffodils, like spots of gold against the dull brown earth, swayed and danced in the massive pots that stood on the paving. Ratty clouds moved quickly around the sun in a patch of blue sky that I could just about see if I craned my neck hard enough.

The kettle shrieked to the boil, bringing me out of my reverie, and as I filled the mugs I thought about the strange dream that I'd had earlier—well, if you could call it a dream. More like an out of body experience, because I really felt as if I had been there—not as an outsider, but one of the people involved, like an actor in some sort of medieval play.

I remembered a lady dressed in a long black gown, and a good-looking man with piercing green eyes and blond hair.

4

Actually, not so different in looks from the "I'm so great" Max Reynolds, who was probably sitting at his desk right now like a king on a throne, waiting for his lowly minion to bring him coffee. Actually, thinking about it, what had Max said earlier? "Methinks you need a shot of caffeine...." Methinks? A sort of ancient, I suppose, medieval saying? Very strange.

Ursula. I suddenly thought. *My name was Ursula.* I had no idea what the lady in the long black gown was called, but I had a sudden memory of the man—whoever he was... the Max Reynolds look-a-like—calling out to her. I thought he had called her my lady, and she had turned around, and then...nothing. Once again a blank; only a fleeting glimpse of her face. Ursula, though. Why did I think I was called Ursula? A strange, old fashioned name.

Putting one of the mugs on my desk, I went through to Max's office, automatically ducking my head under the thick beams that knotted the ceiling, and knocked discreetly before I went in. He was sitting at his desk, everything neat and tidy as usual—a laptop open in front of him, his phone at his side, a pen and a pencil in a straight line. Even files and papers were in pristine little piles. It was a fairly large room for a former cottage, its tiny windows looking out onto the old narrow Havant Road, where a car cruised slowly by.

The rough cream painted walls were bare except for one wall, which featured a large painting of *The Metamorphosis of Narcissus* by Salvador Dali, which I thought suited Max down to the ground. To keep on the same theme, a large oval mirror hung over the fireplace, in which I was sure he preened himself at regular intervals.

Looking at him from under my lashes, I noticed that he looked smart, as he always did for work, wearing a black suit and a white shirt, the top buttons of which were undone, displaying a mat of light curly hair which I studiously ignored, my eyes looking just above his head. Did he really think I was going to fall for that just as all the others did?

I placed the steaming hot mug on a coaster at his side and made to leave the room when Max said, "Feeling okay now, Hannah?"

"Absolutely fine, thank you, boss," I said, edging my way out of the room. "I've got work to do though; I was in the middle of typing up that urgent new will for Mrs. Jordan."

Standing up, Max walked around his desk, although it was more of a prowl than a walk, making me think of a sleek panther. "Hmm. You do know where you are, don't you?"

"Of course I know where I am," I replied irritably.

"Yeah, okay, I know it sounds like a silly question. But you were really out of it just now. You were muttering a name—um...."

Ursula? I thought, then said to Max, "What name?"

"Gregory. Yeah, you said Gregory—very clearly, too. Is he your boyfriend, Hannah? Oh, silly me, you have a boyfriend called Andy, don't you?" A grin swarmed all over his face and his green eyes glittered.

Ignoring the comment about a boyfriend who I'd finished with a while ago, I said, "Max, don't be silly," as I turned once again to leave the room, my hand on the doorknob. "I don't know about you, but I've work to do."

He came nearer and nearer, until he was so close he really was invading my personal space. I could smell the cologne that he wore, sort of oriental and spicy. I took a step back, which unfortunately flattened me against the door.

"As you said, I'm your boss; I need to make sure that you're well enough to be at work. Now just answer a few simple questions, okay?"

Trying to breathe deeply and evenly to calm my erratically beating heart and my temper—which, red hot just behind my eyeballs, was almost at bursting point—I nodded.

"Okay. Now—where are you?"

"I'm at work," I replied as patiently as I could. "At Reynolds & Rhodes, Solicitors, in Havant, Hampshire, situated right next door to the oldest pub in Havant, The Old House at Home." And just for good measure, I added, "There are also branches of Reynolds & Rhodes in Waterlooville and Denmead."

"Great. Correct—with even more information than I needed."

I gave him a scathing glare.

"Now, who is Reynolds and who is Rhodes?"

"Oh, for God's sake, Max." I raised my wrist and tapped pointedly at my watch. Well, my Fitbit, actually. With only three thousand eight hundred steps on it at the moment, which was a disaster, I was sure that at any moment the Fitbit Police would be knocking at the door to take me down to the station for questioning.

"Go on...." He nodded his blond head.

I took a deep, huffing breath. "You are Reynolds. Max Reynolds, the founder of this little enterprise. And Stuart Rhodes is your partner; long-time partner, actually, seeing as you've known each other since bare kneed at school."

"Well done, Hannah. Just one more question. Both Stuart and I have very delightful personal assistants. Who are they?"

Still fuming, and wishing I could get back to my desk and my work, I replied in a very clipped accent—similar, I suppose, to a BBC newsreader back in the day. "I'm your personal assistant, Hannah Palmer, twenty-eight years old, and Stuart's is Sarah Miller, aged twenty-seven, who at this very moment in time is hard at work on her computer—something that I need to be doing right now."

"Excellent, Hannah, full marks. You may go back to your desk and resume your work now that I know you are fully compos mentis."

"Thank you, boss," I snapped.

Max's laughter echoed in the very air around me as I stalked back to my office.

The will that I'd been typing before my strange experience occurred was still on the screen just as I'd left it. The words in curly black script, "This is the last Will and Testament" jumped out at me, as in this case did the name of the dog that was due to come into a fortune. Mr. Al Pacino—what a name for a pet. Mrs. Jordan must surely be a massive Pacino fan. I supposed, though, that it made a good change from Rex or Tiddles, or border collies named Molly.

I took a sip of coffee, which was now lukewarm, thanks to Max. If he hadn't kept me in his office for so long, I'd have been enjoying a hot drink now. What an irritating man he could be at times. Admittedly, he was a good boss—very fair, and kind even, and he had a great sense of humor. But when it came to the opposite sex, he turned into some sort of juvenile delinquent. He'd had so many girlfriends in the year I'd been working for him that I'd lost count.

Thank God I didn't look like his usual type, willowy and blonde with big baby blue eyes. In fact, I was the exact opposite, having shoulder length dark hair and hazel eyes. My figure, while not being fat, was definitely not willowy. Maybe that was why I'd gotten the job as his PA, so he wouldn't be tempted to flirt with me. Not, as I'd thought at the time, because of my qualifications and experience as a super legal secretary.

Putting that aside, though, and forgetting about his romantic life, it could be said that he'd done really well for himself. Having his own very successful law firm at only thirty-two was quite an achievement, and if I had any other hat than that old decrepit beanie that I wore when the weather was really cold, I would certainly take it off to him.

"Hey, Hannah." Sarah came out of her office, dressed in virtually the same outfit as me — a black trouser suit teamed with a red blouse, the only difference being that my blouse was green. "Hey, you okay?" she asked.

I raised a hand as she disappeared into the kitchen, no doubt to make a revitalizing cup of coffee. I followed her and stood in the doorway, leaning against the door jamb as I filled her in on my weird experience that morning.

She chuckled as she put coffee into a mug and added hot water, and then milk. "Hey, ooh...you're not turning into Margaret Pole, are you?"

I frowned. "Margaret Pole? Who on earth is Margaret Pole?"

"Hey, you don't know?"

I shook my head, wondering not for the first time why Sarah started every sentence with the word hey. Maybe she thought it sounded hip? But "hey," she was a good friend to me, and even though we'd only gotten to know each other through working at the solicitors' office, we actually lived together.

Don't get the wrong idea — neither of us were gay. It was just the only way that both of us could afford to buy a house and finally be in a position to leave home. We'd decided to pool our resources, and now lived in an ex-council house on Mitchell Road in Bedhampton — number forty, to be exact. It was all working really well so far, and we shared everything —

the bills, the house work, even the gardening. Sarah's boyfriend, Neil, was a regular visitor, but I was keeping away from men at the moment after the disaster that was Andy just a few months ago. Max had no idea that we had finished, and I still didn't really want to talk about my ex.

Anyway, I zoned back to the conversation with Sarah, who was valiantly trying to get my attention.

"Hey, Hannah?"

"Oh, sorry, Sarah. Yeah, who was Margaret Pole?"

"Hey, she was the cousin or second cousin — or something like that — of Henry the Eighth."

"Really? Wow. But why should my experience have anything to do with her?"

"Hey." Cradling her mug in both hands, she leaned back against the work top, comfortably crossing her legs at the ankles, and said, "Well, local history, you know. She lived in Warblington Castle, or Warblington Manor as it's usually called — you know, the ruin by the cemetery? — for the last twenty or so years of her life. Henry visited her there, and apparently actually gave her the manor in fifteen thirteen. There's only a turret left, which was part of the old gate house."

She took a sip of her drink while I waited with bated breath for the next installment. I looked at her intently — at her pretty face, freckles covering her nose like a dot to dot drawing, her highlighted bobbed hair, and her beautiful, almond shaped eyes.

"Henry the Eighth visited her there?" I said. "That's amazing." An image came into my mind of the old ruin near the church at Warblington, just a turret sticking up into the sky. I'd never seen it up close because it was on private land and hard to get to.

10

"Hey, apparently, he had her executed for treason—his own cousin or second cousin or whatever—and she was really old for Tudor times…sixty-seven and very frail. What a cruel man he was."

"Well," I replied, "He had a couple of his own wives executed, so I suppose a cousin would be nothing to him."

"Hey, yeah, you're right there. But he had at one time been really close to her. She was royal governess to his kids, and even godmother to Mary—Bloody Mary, as she went on to be. Anyway, better get on." She took her phone from her pocket and glanced at it for the time—more and more people seemed to not wear watches these days, except Fitbits, of course—and then took a sip of her drink. "Stuart will be back from court soon, and I promised I'd have all his letters ready for him to sign."

"How do you know all this stuff about Henry the Eighth and Margaret Pole?" I asked as we went back into the office.

"Hey, studied history, particularly the Tudors, at college," Sarah replied, then went on to say, "Hey, you'll have to Google Margaret Pole. Interesting reading, particularly because of it being local. I think she had kids too, four boys and a girl. Poor girl, having four brothers." She made a woeful face and I laughed at her. "Hey, I think her daughter was called Ursula. Cool name, don't you think?"

I stared after her open mouthed, thinking of the lady in the long black gown—who the good-looking Max Reynolds look-a-like had called "my lady" —and this weird feeling that I was called Ursula. Coincidence or what?

Sitting back at my desk—my interest in Margaret Pole at the forefront of my mind—and being very naughty, I minimized the urgent will for Mrs. Jordan (temporarily of course), and reaching for my mouse, clicked decisively on

Google Chrome.

~*~

The carriage lurched and swayed its way along the deeply rutted road to Warblington Manor. Thank God the rain had kept away, otherwise the day's journey from Havant to Langstone would have been virtually impossible, and I would never have reached home tonight. Two gleaming black horses pulled the carriage, the muscles in their necks straining with the effort, their hooves slipping and stumbling on the slippery mud. They neighed anxiously as the driver's whip arched through the air, slicing into their sweating backs.

A strong smell of horse flesh hung in the air, mingling most unpleasantly with the ripe odor of the driver who held tightly to the reins, his fingernails black as coal. I held a crisp starched handkerchief over my nose, my initials UP—for Ursula Pole—monogrammed in tiny swirling stitches in one corner.

Hanging on for dear life to the stout leather straps fixed to the carriage roof, I peered from the tiny window at the pretty Hampshire countryside, at the green fields that, because it was spring, were a mass of golden daffodils and rapeseed, at the leafy green trees, and at the arching blue sky dotted with patchy grey clouds. I cranked the window down a little and took a deep breath, inhaling air that was fresh and sweet after the musty interior of the carriage.

The carriage rattled along the driveway now, slightly flatter and smoother than the pot holed turnpike, trees curving above us making a mysterious leafy green tunnel. I caught glimpses of the house between the trees; solid, four storied, with imposing turrets at each corner and tiny mullioned windows glinting in the sunshine.

Suddenly the gardens opened up around us, showing

clipped lawns and borders filled with a mass of forget me nots and black-eyed Susans. We passed a lone gardener digging into the earth with a shiny spade. He glanced up, eyes narrowed, as we lurched past, a breeze tousling his blond hair and flattening his white shirt against a hairy muscular chest.

My mother, Margaret Pole, appeared in the shadowy doorway to welcome me. An imposing figure, she wore a square necked richly embroidered scarlet gown, her dark hair hidden beneath a hood that rose slightly on her head like a little house, making her appear taller than she actually was. She walked regally down the front steps, silken scarlet shoes peeking from the hem of her gown.

"Ursula, darling." She hugged me so close that that I could detect a sweet rose scent emanating from her skin and her clothes.

"My lady." I curtseyed, giving a tiny bow of my head as I did so.

"Lovely to see you, sweetheart. Come, come…."

She grasped my hand and led me inside and into a dark stone flagged hallway, and from there into the great hall where my father, Sir Richard Pole, stood in front of the massive fireplace.

A fire burned in the grate, sulky and smoking, filling the huge room with a grey haze. The tantalizing smell of roasting meat wafted from the kitchens. Two of my brothers, Reginald and Geoffrey, sat on hard wooden benches dressed in doublet and hose, looking as extravagantly bright as a couple of strutting peacocks. My father's dogs, Gilbert and Sturdy, slumbered as close to the fire as they could possibly get.

"Ah. Little Bear." My father held out his arms, into which I gladly fell before stepping back and curtseying deeply, my somber gown belling around me like a pool of dark water.

"My lord," The meaning of the name Ursula and my father's use of my nickname "Little Bear" made me smile.

"Did you have a good visit with Abigail?" he asked, Abigail being a childhood friend who I'd been staying with in nearby Emsworth.

"Yes, Father—" I began, when I was rudely interrupted by my brother, Geoffrey, who looked up quickly at the mention of my friend.

"Abigail? When is she visiting here?"

This question was met with wild laughter from Reginald, and the statement, "Ah yes, the fair Abigail, eh Geoffrey?"

I knew that Geoffrey was sweet on Abigail and she on him, as she had mentioned him many times throughout my visit. I had no doubt that if of benefit to both families a match would be made there. Geoffrey blushed to the very roots of his hair, making Reginald laugh even more.

My mother touched my arm and said, "Come, Ursula, I'll go with you to your room before dinner is served."

Picking up my travelling bag, I followed my mother's swaying figure up the wide stone staircase to the floor above, stopping briefly on the large rectangular landing to peer from the tiny slit of a window. The gardener was still out there busily digging, his spade glinting in the sunshine and the muscles in his strong arms working furiously. I stood on my tiptoes so that I could get a better view. I wondered who he was and what he was called. I'd never seen him working in our garden before.

He must have felt my gaze on him, for suddenly he stopped working and, brushing a lock of blond hair from his forehead, stared up at me, his eyes narrowed and glinting green. Quickly I turned away, expecting to see my mother waiting for me at my bedchamber door, but instead was met with darkness. I reached out a hand but there was nothing — only the dark, a deep, deep blackness — and then my stomach rolled and twisted as I began to fall.

Chapter Two

Fumbling around in the darkness, my hands encountered what felt surprisingly like brooms and dust pans and brushes that clattered loudly as I knocked against them. Rough walls surrounded me, and something sticky—ugh, not a spider's web. —touched my hair. Where was I and, come to that, where was my mother? She'd disappeared so suddenly. The door swung open, making me narrow my eyes against a shaft of bright sunlight showing not my mother, Margaret Pole, as I had expected, but the puzzled face of Max Reynolds, Stuart Rhodes peering over his shoulder like a rubbernecker.

"What on earth are you doing, Hannah?" asked Max. Frowning, he gazed at me, probably wondering what on earth I was doing groping around in the dark in the broom cupboard, a place that even I didn't expect to be in.

Feeling disorientated but coming quickly to my senses, I replied, "Oh, I broke my mug and needed the dustpan and brush. There's pieces of china around my desk, all over the carpet—"

"You look really pale," remarked Stuart, a frown puckering his forehead. "Here, give me the brush and I'll clear it up for you."

He reached out his hand. I hesitated, picturing my desk and the clean, recently Hoovered carpet with not even a tiny piece of china in sight. The cleaning lady always did a good job, even leaving the long narrow marks of the Hoover attachment on the pile.

"Oh my God. Do you know what?" I said, slapping my forehead with my palm like an actor in a bad comedy as I sidled out of the cupboard and shut the door with a click. "I was in the cupboard putting the brush away, not getting it out." Because of Max and Stuart's blank looks, I gabbled on, adding, "I'm losing it," while throwing my head back and laughing manically.

Both men followed me back to the office, and both stood hesitantly in the doorway as I made myself comfortable at my desk and prepared to finally get on with some work. I glanced at them from the corner of my eye. Max looked so tall and blond compared to Stuart's swarthy darkness and shorter stature.

"I'm fine," I assured them, waving airily, trying to cover up how shaky and sick I really felt.

Max prowled around my desk, inspecting the carpet, then looked at me suspiciously. "Hmm. Well, whatever you broke, you did a really good clean up job."

"Well," I replied. "I'm a woman—I'm good at cleaning."

"No sexist comments around here, please," commented Stuart with a grin.

Max stared at me for what seemed like ages, his green eyes glinting, before saying, "I'd go to the ladies' room if I were you, Hannah."

"Yeah," agreed Stuart. "I've got to agree with Max. You look as though you've been living in a deep, dark, very dirty cave for about six months."

Max then put out his hand and picked up a mug from my desk. "Broke your mug did you, Hannah?"

I looked at my favorite mug, the mug that I always used, "World's Greatest Daughter" imprinted in thick black letters around its smooth surface. Quick as a flash I replied, "I was using a different mug...for once."

Max shook his head very slowly, very suspiciously, and then, glancing at each other and chuckling, both men disappeared from the doorway.

Hmm, close call, I thought, glancing at the unbroken mug standing so innocently on my desk. Standing up, I made my way to the ladies' room, taking my makeup bag with me.

The mirror showed a pale face streaked with dust and dirt, and what actually did look like sticky spider's webs coating my hair like a net. Cringing, I brushed it away, and then, with shaking fingers, splashed my face with cold water. Now I looked totally ridiculous, with black streaks all around my eyes so that I resembled a rather sad looking panda. I took a long deep breath, the sickness abating now, yet still leaving me shaky and disorientated.

What must Max and Stuart have thought? Did they really believe the story about the broken mug? I wouldn't have thought so, and certainly not with me suddenly appearing from the broom cupboard looking as if I'd stepped out of a horror movie. Thank God Max hadn't asked to have a look at the broken mug. What would I have done then? It didn't bear thinking about.

Did I really care what Max thought anyway? Max who didn't even recognize me from an encounter that we'd once had. Yeah, okay it was years before I worked for him, but to be erased totally from his memory and not even be recognized when I came for the interview was a bit hard to take, even though I knew him straight away. Closing my eyes, I was back there in that hot sweaty night club, my friends pointing and laughing when Max approached me for a dance. I'd had far too much to drink, the wine had been flowing copiously that night, and Max, tall good-looking Max, had appeared, it seemed, from nowhere, grabbing me hard around the waist and pulling me close to him.

My heart still skipped a bit as I remembered his beautiful green eyes staring into mine as we shuffled around the dance floor, the words of the song "You to me Are Everything" still imprinted on my brain even now. He'd whispered sweet things, his breath tickling my ear; that I was beautiful, my dark hair and eyes were gorgeous, that I had a lovely smile, and that he wanted to see me again. His lips were close, tantalizingly close, but we didn't kiss. I gave him my phone number scribbled on a damp beer mat, which he stupidly kissed with a flourish and put carefully into the back pocket of his trousers. I noticed that a girl, legs grazing her arm pits, long blonde hair falling like a stream over her shoulders, rushed over and clung onto his arm as he strode back to the bar, back to his friends. Huh. Shouldn't that have been a heads up for me about his Barbies?

I didn't get a call from him, even though night after night I waited and waited for the phone to ring. It had been difficult working for him at times, especially when he irritated me so unbearably, but I'd never reminded him of that night — it would be too embarrassing, as it had so obviously meant nothing to him. So, knowing full well what sort of a man he was — a man I could never become involved with — and also not wanting to pass up such a good job, I was hopeful that I could put the past behind me and concentrate on the future as boss and personal assistant, and so far it was working fine.

19

Forcing myself out of dreams of the past and putting them firmly behind me, I stared at myself in the mirror, wondering what on earth was going on in my life now. Was Sarah right? Was I turning into Margaret Pole? Well, not Margaret, but her daughter, Ursula? I thought of the woman who had come out of what I assumed was Warblington Manor to greet me, my mother; well, my mother in a previous life as Ursula Pole. Was that what it was? Had I really lived a previous life? Did I believe in all that stuff? Both Margaret Pole and Warblington Manor looked pretty much the same as the pictures I'd seen of them on the Internet, uncannily so. It couldn't all be in my imagination, surely.

Oh my God, I suddenly remembered the information that I'd found out when reading about Ursula Pole on Wikipedia. Apparently she had had fourteen children — seven boys and seven girls. Good God, was I going to have to go through her life and give birth to all those children? That didn't even bear thinking about.

I decided that when I finished work that evening I would go to Warblington Church and have a close look at the ruins of Warblington Castle or Warblington Manor — whatever it was called. I needed to get close to it, touch the stones, and maybe get some vibes. Vibes? What was I on about? Yeah, okay, I was definitely losing it.

I looked intently into the mirror and, with some damp tissue, scrubbed at my face again to get rid of the black marks around my eyes. I applied a slick of lip gloss, and then, taking a deep breath, went back to my desk and tried to get on with some work. Hey, Mrs. Jordan's will was calling to me — and a dog called Mr. Al Pacino.

~*~

Needles of hot sunshine burned into my skin as I turned

my face to the sun like a flower desperate for light. The area around my eyes felt oddly stiff and sore and I ran my fingers gently over my skin, feeling my cheek, which was puffy and swollen. When I tried to open my eyes, one opened only to a slit. I gazed around, my good eye taking in my surroundings.

I was sitting on a stone bench in a beautiful walled garden. My soft green slippers rested on a paved path surrounded by emerald lawns and oval flower beds that rioted with spring blooms in all the colors of the rainbow—bright pink and red, lemon and orange, a splash of violet and cerise. The smell of freshly cut grass slid into my nostrils.

Glancing down, I noticed that I wore a long green gown richly embroidered with tiny even stitches. *Who made this?* I thought. Elves, fairies, goblins? Who else could embroider with such delicate stitches? Small hands were needed for this intricate work. The day was far too hot for the gown which was made of a heavy silk, and I felt stifled encased in its thick confines.

I drifted, dreaming, my hands resting on the small mound of my stomach. Then, while caressing the mound, I could feel something inside moving, rocking and rolling, and I became aware of tiny flutters, like the trapped wing of a bird.

The flutters made me breathless, and suddenly, with an almost sickening clarity, I realized that I wasn't Hannah Palmer any more—a legal secretary working for Max Reynolds, and whose parents were Bill and Marjorie, who had a sister, Claire, and a brother, Ryan, who loved marmite but hated honey, and really enjoyed a glass of red wine and just loved Tamla Motown and the Kooks, and was trying really hard to get into fitness—but that I was Ursula Pole, the daughter of Sir Richard Pole and Margaret Pole, and that I was pregnant, around four or five months pregnant by the look of it. Was

21

this my first child? Or my second, my third — my fourteenth?
Oh my God.

"Ursula?"

A deep sexy voice brought me out of my reverie, and
looking up I came face to face with the very attractive blond
gardener who I had spied from the window the last time I
had been here as Ursula. He bore such a striking resemblance
to the "I'm so great" Max Reynolds that confusion reigned in
my mind and I had to take a deep breath to steady myself.

He was clad, as before, in black trousers tied loosely at
the waist, and a white shirt that was stretched taut across his
muscular chest, his hands resting on his slim hips. He gazed
at me intently, then suddenly, with a heartfelt sigh, he sank
down onto the bench, saying, "Dear God, Ursula, what has he
done? What has he done to your face?"

He grabbed my hands, which looked tiny enveloped in his
large ones, and pulled me close. I melted into him, smelling
his special familiar smell, not new and clean like the odor I
had smelled from Max, but something else, from another time
perhaps — horses, hay, and tobacco.

"Who?" I asked him in a panic. "Who has done what to
my face?"

"Why, Henry of course," he replied. Pulling slightly away
from me, he frowned, his hands on my shoulders. "Henry,
your husband. Have you not looked at your face, Ursula?"

"My husband?" I asked him. "But then how…?" I gestured
towards him, and he smiled and pulled back further to look
properly at me. I noticed that his eyes glowed like emeralds
in his face.

"Yes, it's wrong. You're a married noble woman, and I
just a lowly gardener. But it began a long time before you
were wed. It's like a drug, our love, like a drug that we can't

22

give up."

Gently he laced his fingers with mine, squeezing my hand, his eyes never leaving my face. I smiled and nodded, agreeing with him, imagining—no, not imagining, but knowing, really knowing—what it was like, this affair, this love affair. He pulled me close, so close that my cheek rubbed against his, and I felt his stubbly beard, and knew without a doubt that this wasn't just an infatuation, but that I had been intimate with this man. That I had kissed his lips, that he had lain on top of me, had caressed me, touched me, made love to me. And I knew his name was Gregory, Gregory Walsh, and that he was thirty-two years old and unmarried.

I knew that he had his father still, but that his mother was dead and lay deep in the earth in Warblington Cemetery. Her stone was in the shape of a heart, engraved with cherished memories, and he went faithfully every week to lay flowers on her grave. Was this child his? Oh, how glad I would be if it were. My free hand was drawn again to my stomach and I rubbed it gently.

"Have you pains?" he asked tenderly. "This is your first time, dear one. Are you comfortable?"

"No, no pains," I assured him. "I'm very comfortable." Then I added, "Is this baby my husband's?"

"You seem to think so," he replied sadly, and then glanced at me quizzically, narrowing his eyes, saying brusquely, "You have assured me of dates and times...."

I nodded, knowing that I must be careful. I was asking too many questions. I didn't want him to have even a tiny inkling that I wasn't really Ursula Pole and that my name was Hannah Palmer, and that I was living a perfectly ordinary life five hundred or so years into the future. What on earth would he say to that? He would think me deranged.

23

To pacify him, I said, "Henry has vowed he will not strike me again, and with the help of my brothers I do not think he will."

"Your brothers?" he asked.

"They will defend me, dear Gregory — as will my father."

We sat in a companionable silence for a while, then Gregory said, "I've heard your father call you Little Bear. What does this mean, Ursula?"

"It is the meaning of my name, Ursula," I told him. "A nickname only."

He smiled at this, and then, clasping my hands in his, said, "Oh Ursula, with all my being, I too will try to protect you from Henry Stafford. I will not have him do this to you again."

I gazed at his face, at his lovely, kind face. I knew that his words were pure and true, and when I replied I said, "Oh, Gregory, I know that you will, and feel comforted by this."

I thought back to what he had said earlier. *My first baby — my first one out of fourteen.*

My heart sank at what the future would bring and I turned to him again, to Gregory, to put my head against his chest, to feel the wild beating of his heart, to talk to him again and to tell him that I was afraid that Henry would take back his words and strike me again. But he wasn't there. There was nobody there, only my computer standing on the smooth wooden desk, the tiny cursor beating against the screen, against the words of Mrs. Jordan's still unfinished will, such a poor replacement for the warm pulse of Gregory Walsh.

Sitting rigidly on the edge of my leather swivel chair, I bent at the waist, my face cupped in my hands, waiting until the sickness passed and the room stopped rotating like a seventies silver disco ball.

Chapter Three

Max gave me a cheery wave from the open window of his silver Mondeo as he drove expertly from the parking lot after work that evening. I noticed that a swathe of long blonde hair cascaded over the passenger seat, but however much I craned my neck, I couldn't be sure that it was the same girl that he had been wining and dining last week, or the week before.

Sarah and I called it, jokingly of course, and certainly not to his face, "The Barbie Doll Syndrome." That was his type, I supposed—impossibly long legs, long blonde hair, tanned skin, tiny tight outfits. Sarah and I were keeping our fingers crossed that Max didn't suddenly turn into Barbie's boyfriend, Ken. Now that would be a disaster.

Remembering that I'd said I'd go to the cemetery after work to get vibes from the stones of the ruin of Warblington Manor, and hopefully to shed some light on the weird dreams that I'd been having, I pulled out of the parking lot in my pride and joy, Daphne the red Mini, and made my way through Havant town center. People in a rush to get home from work scurried along the pavements, school kids dawdled, their rucksacks hanging untidily from their backs, and little children cried, red faced, and dragged their feet even as they clung to the comfort of mummy or daddy.

I drove past Streets Ironmongers, where I remembered going with my grandmother, or Nan, when I was a little girl. She had loved that place. It was all closed up and derelict now, which made me feel really nostalgic. I smiled to myself as I remembered us being together, me and Nan, our shoes tapping on the wooden floors amidst the stifling smell of paint and airy, choking sawdust. I remembered sifting through smooth shiny nails and screws, and being fascinated by thick, shiny green hose pipe and the delicate leaves of plants, their roots buried in rich dark soil.

My Nan had been such a tiny woman, barely reaching my shoulder when I was a teenager, that it was difficult to believe that she had given birth to ten children. My mum, Marjorie, was one of ten. So really, was it so shocking that Ursula's offspring had reached the unbelievable number of fourteen?

Mulling this over, my head spinning, I drove slowly by the Bear public house and Empire Court, a block of flats that had been built on the old footprint of the Empire Cinema, where my mum and dad had met many years before. I shook my head as I remembered Dad's words when I had asked what he had first noticed about Mum, "I liked your mum's backside in her tight black skirt."

Smiling to myself, I sped past the turn off to Southleigh Road and Warblington School. Even at this time, school kids were still milling about outside the one stop shop at the bottom of the road as I drove past and on to Warblington Cemetery.

Even though it wasn't dark yet, the orange glow of streetlights lit up Church Lane as I parked in the small parking lot in front of St Thomas à Becket Church. The church, squatting low in the approaching gloom like a steepled hand, was surrounded by old mildew encrusted gravestones that leaned wearily, and a massive yew tree, its branches whispering in the breeze as they brushed against the church's ancient stones. I wrinkled my nose at the stench of muddy sea from nearby Langstone, or "Langstone on the Mud," as people call it.

As I got out of the car a sudden cold gust of wind made me shiver, and I hunched down into the warmth of my coat, put my gloved hands into my pockets, and walked with purpose back down the lane. As I hurried by I glanced down Pook Lane, which I had been told was haunted by ghosts and ghoulies, and walked away from the cemetery, to where, hopefully, I would be nearer to the ruins of Warblington Manor.

I could see it as I approached—a turret pointing up into the sky, a sky which was now neither light nor dark but something in between, an inky blue with wispy skeins of clouds being pushed around as if by an invisible hand in the strengthening wind. I could see the imprint of thousands of tiny stars preparing to shine, and the moon waiting on the horizon.

The first thing I noticed as I got closer to the ruins was that the gate, a sturdy looking wooden affair, was open, wide open. I'd never seen it that way before, and hesitated momentarily. But then I thought, *Private land or not, I'm going in; this is important*, before walking quickly through and along a smooth tarmacked path. Beyond the ruin I could see a rather more modern manor house surrounded by large colorful gardens, with a couple of mud splattered SUVs parked outside.

A shallow depression in the moist earth, which I assume had once been the moat, surrounded the turret, through which I tiptoed carefully, trying not to get my boots dirty, as the mud, still sticky and squelchy, had not quite dried from the winter. Close to the ruin now, I gazed up at the imposing structure of red brick and stone, the top of which seemed to disappear into the clouds, it was so high. I could see tiny slits of windows, and I almost expected Rapunzel to appear and hang down her golden hair so I may climb it like a stair. I smiled to myself as I thought how easy it would be for one of Max's girlfriends to help with that.

Dusk was beginning to fall and the sky arched above me, twinkling now with stars and the moon, which hung motionless like a silver globe. Pulling off my gloves, I placed my hands on the cold stones of the turret and closed my eyes. I counted down slowly from ten to one. Nothing happened. Furtively I glanced around, hoping that nobody was watching me, that nobody was peering from the tiny windows of the nearby manor house and wondering who I was and what I was doing there. I was very conscious that I shouldn't be there, that I was on private land and that the owners had every right to ask me to leave if they wanted to.

A light flicked on in one of the downstairs rooms, a rosy welcoming glow shining through the window. I caught a glimpse of a large squashy sofa and a fluffy orange rug in front of a fireplace big enough to sit in. I pressed my cold hands into the stone again and closed my eyes, taking deep even breaths as I did so.

My heart thumped hard against my ribs as I became aware suddenly of a change in the air, from a slight chill to balmy, and the stones of the ruin felt warm beneath my palms. Birds chirped and squawked, and soft green leaves appeared on the trees. I smiled as I took another deep breath and inhaled what was now a stifling summer's day. Then I heard the sound of heavy marching boots.

"No," shrieked a voice, a female voice. "No, you can't do

this. No, no, no…."

Quick as a flash I turned around to see my mother, Margaret Pole — older now than the last time I'd seen her, her face etched with wrinkles — being forcibly dragged from the shadowy doorway of Warblington Manor by several burly men dressed in uniform. Somehow the ruin had disappeared and the intact structure, the old manor house, stood there in all its glory.

She writhed and struggled in their strong grip, her dainty slippers dragging along the path, their pretty decorative stones falling off and shining like silver droplets on the ground. But they held on tightly with their massive hands, and I could imagine that even through the thick folds of her gown bruises would bloom that night on her shoulders and her arms.

"It's under the orders of the king, my lady," one of the men informed her. He was broad chested and stocky, his arms and legs solid and thick. A straggly beard sprouted from a chin that jutted like stone, and his eyes, light blue and hard, stared at her, uncaring.

"The king?" she questioned, panic struck. "Henry? My Henry?" She glanced sideways at the man, her nostrils flaring with either anger or terror. I'd never seen that expression on her face before.

"Yes, my lady," he replied reverently. "King Henry the Eighth of England." He bowed his head slightly as he said the king's name, still holding on tightly to my mother.

The other men nodded their heads and echoed his words as they carried on dragging her towards a black carriage, emblazoned with the king's arms that stood waiting at the huge gates beyond the moat. Two shiny black horses, spattered with mud and sweating in the hot sunshine, pawed the ground impatiently with their dangerous hooves.

Still struggling in their grasp, my mother said breathlessly, "I need to speak with him. Tell the king I need to speak with him. Henry will listen, he is my kin. I am all alone here today. My husband is not within, and my sons are away." As if grasping for straws, she said with a whimper, "My daughter, Ursula, will come for me, but she is busy. The children—she has so many children."

It was a warm day here in the 1500s, the sky a bright blue with no clouds, and I squinted against the sun, my mother and the soldiers a red blur, as I thought, *Should I show myself? If I do, will she be able see me?*

With my arms outstretched, I began to step towards her, my mother, who, distraught at such barbarism, had slid to the ground onto her poor arthritic knees and was openly crying, glassy tears falling down her face. Impervious to her pleas, the soldiers continued to drag her towards the carriage, her beautiful gown shredding on the rough ground, blood now seeping from cuts and scratches on her spindly legs.

I called to her over and over again, "Mother, Mother," but she didn't seem to hear, nor did she see me as I approached her and the bunch of foul soldiers. "Get away from her." I shouted at them. "Get away." But they seemed not to see me and carried on with their terrible work, pushing her roughly into the carriage like a sack of potatoes and slamming the door. The carriage rattled away, lurching from side to side like a drunk. Helplessly I watched it go, my hands clasped to my breast to still the hurried beating of my heart. I was so afraid that I would never see her again.

I turned at the sound of a voice, and with such gladness saw Gregory and promptly threw myself into his arms. "Oh, darling," I said. "I'm so glad you're here."

He didn't reply but just stared at me, taking in all my

30

features, so it seemed — my eyes, my lips, his bright green gaze resting on my mouth for what seemed an eternity. Then his sumptuous lips came down on mine and we kissed passionately, clinging tightly together like vines.

Not wanting to, but common-sense taking hold and remembering the plight of my mother, I pulled away, breathless, and whispered urgently, "Oh dear one, you must help me. You must help my mother; the soldiers have taken her on the orders of the king."

His answer surprised me. "Hannah?" He grabbed my shoulders in his hands. "What are you saying? Are you delirious? What soldiers? What on earth are you talking about?"

The whole world seemed to tilt on its axis and I spun around and around like the spinning top that I'd played with as a little girl, until everything was a blur. Gradually the earth began to slow and I became aware that the heat had gone, that the sun no longer blazed from a clear blue sky, and that it was cold and dusky here in my time. Here in my little corner of the world.

Then the earth slowed further and further until it was still, and I was able to look at the man whose strong arms encircled me, and I saw with a growing disbelief that it wasn't Gregory as I had thought. It was Max, my boss Max Reynolds, and he was staring at me open mouthed as if I'd lost my mind.

~*~

"Yes, I know, Claire," I said. "Mum told me that you're working part time in a baker's shop. Smith & Vosper, isn't it?"

"Yeah, in Havant town center. You know, just by — "

"Yes, I know where it is — next door to Woolworths — "

"I didn't really want to go back to legal work, Hannah," she butted in lamely. "I'm enjoying the baker's, doing

31

something different."

"It's only for a few months," I told her. "Just until Sarah's better. Otherwise we'll have to advertise, and it's a pain, you know. Anyway, whatever, Max asked me to have a word with you. 'Ask your little sister,' he said. 'We know that she's a super-efficient legal secretary.' But never mind."

There was a slight pause before she said, "Well, if I did — and I said if...," she pointed out. "It could only be part time. I want to carry on working at the baker's."

I grinned to myself. I knew I could get around her eventually, especially if I bulled her up and told her how good she was. We were struggling in the office though, as Sarah had suddenly gone off sick with shingles, and might be absent from work for at least a couple of months. We needed all the help we could get.

"Part time is great," I told her. "Come in and see Max, have a chat with him."

"Hmm," she replied. "I'm not sure about working with Max; he's a bit up himself, isn't he?"

I laughed loudly and imagined Claire pulling her mobile away from her ear and looking at it in disgust. "You don't have to worry about that, Claire, I work for Max. You'd be working for Stuart, and he's a good guy, although Max is okay too, really."

"An acquired taste," she said disdainfully.

Laughing to myself, I clicked off my mobile and laid it beside me on the desk. We'd arranged for her to call in to see Max and Stuart the very next day. I was sure she would take the job. It would be good to work with Claire. I'd missed her while she'd been working as a legal secretary in London, and to have her here even part time would be a great help. I'd been struggling the past week with Sarah's workload as well as mine, and it was really getting to me. Also, it didn't help that things had been a bit strained between me and Max since our strange encounter in Warblington Cemetery the week before.

I didn't understand the kiss that we had shared, and I was sure that Max was totally regretting it, as he had pulled away immediately, and ever since had been distant from me, hostile even. I knew that I had a lot of explaining to do for what I had said to him about Margaret Pole, the soldiers, and the king, but I wasn't sure where to start. Knowing Max, he would laugh if I told him about the strange dreams that I was having, the dreams that seemed so real.

I suppose that the only explanation I could give him for the kiss was that I mistook him for Gregory Walsh; they looked so much alike. But having to tell Max that I thought he was a man that I'd encountered hundreds of years back in time would, no doubt, also be met with ridicule.

Anyway, if I'd known that it was Max and not Gregory that I was with, the kiss would never have happened. I had no feelings whatsoever for Max in that way and, although it had been very enjoyable, I was absolutely sure that I'd only liked it so much because I'd thought it was Gregory that I was kissing and not Max. Yes, that was definitely the case. Most definitely. Wasn't it?

Also, I had yet to find out what Max had been doing in the cemetery that evening. What had he been up to? I made up my mind then and there that next time I had a chance to speak to him alone, I would ask the question.

Anyway, since then nothing had happened, nothing at all. No trips back in time, and I was desperate to find out what had happened to my mother—well, I mean Ursula Pole's mother—after being taken away by that pack of ruthless soldiers. I dreaded that if it happened again, if I ever did go back again, it would be to witness her execution, and from what I had read on Wikipedia it had been a terribly gruesome sight.

Also, I wanted to see Gregory — I longed to see Gregory. I longed for the smell of him, the sweet citrusy scent of his skin, the feel of his stubbly beard against my cheek, and the beat of his heart against mine. I felt that I was in love with him. But how could I be in love with a man who had lived centuries before, and was now nothing but dust?

I had googled Gregory Walsh, frantically googled him, hoping and praying that something would come up on the screen of my computer, but had found nothing. There was no information about him at all, and as each day went by, I was conscious of the fact that he was living somewhere back in time, living and breathing through each and every day without me.

That is, I thought with a sickening jolt, *If he ever lived at all, and wasn't just a figment of my imagination.* I reassured myself with the fact that I couldn't be imagining Margaret or Ursula; that they had lived, that they had been real, as had Henry, my husband. I'd read all about them on Wikipedia. Maybe there was no information about Gregory because he had lived as just an ordinary man, that he wasn't royal or related to royalty as Margaret and Ursula were.

Coming out of my reverie, I heard the tread of footsteps coming across the tiled entrance way floor, and suspected that it was Max coming to check up on me, checking that I was getting on with my work, and he probably wanted to know what Claire had said about covering for Sarah. Well, I had news for him on that score. Good news as well; and maybe it would be the ideal time to talk to him properly about what had happened that evening in the cemetery.

I gazed at my computer screen, at the document laid out before me—another will, but that's what came from working in probate. This time it was the last will and testament for a Mr. Michael Strothers, who was leaving everything to his daughter, Michaela—his house, his car, all his money, everything. Lucky Michaela.

I glanced at the door, wondering when Max was actually going to make an appearance, as it seemed ages since I'd heard footfalls in the hallway. But all was quiet and all was still. I frowned as I noticed that the light was fading, and glancing at my Fitbit—still with very few steps on it—saw that it was only four o'clock in the afternoon. But the small paved area, so bright yellow with daffodils just a few minutes earlier, was dusky now and shadowy, the flowers shining in the gloom like a child's night light. I realized that I would have to switch on the office lights if I wanted to see what I was doing, which was very strange for this time of day in April.

All of a sudden the office door, which had been so firmly closed, screeched open, making me jump. To my total surprise it wasn't Max that came rushing towards me in a panic, but my mother, Margaret Pole. She looked tired and drawn, the skin beneath her eyes a puffy pale blue, and her hair, normally pulled back briskly or covered in a sumptuous hood, was soft and relaxed, with tiny wispy tendrils framing her face. She looked strange, diminished almost without the height of the hood, without the tiny peaked house on top of her head.

"Ursula," she said. "Oh Ursula, let me help you, my dear one."

My heart beating as hard as a drum, I stood up and noticed straight away a faint irritating needling pain in the small of my back. My heart thumping heavily like a drum, I held out my hands to my mother, who grabbed them like a lifeline.

35

Then, to my utmost dismay, I felt water sliding slowly down my soft inner thighs and pooling around my bare feet, like a thick gluey scab on what had suddenly become old bumpy floorboards.

Putting my hands gently on the writhing bump that had so recently been Hannah Palmer's somewhat flatter stomach, I realized with a heavy heart that my pregnancy was coming to an end, that I was in labor, and that today I, Ursula Pole, would give birth to my first child, a son, who would be named Henry after his father, and also after the king.

Chapter Four

Max raised his glass of sparkling white wine and we all followed suit, Claire, Stuart and I, clinking our glasses against one another's in the soft genial atmosphere of The Old House at Home public house. Max had arranged this evening to celebrate the fact that my sister, Claire, would be coming to work with us on a temporary part time basis. He had done the same for both Sarah and I at the start of our employment.

"Thanks, Claire, for agreeing to help us out on such short notice," said Max, taking a sip from his drink. "I don't think you realize how stretched we've been without Sarah."

"Hmm, tell me about it," I said. "I've been run ragged."

"Yes," said Stuart. "Hannah can now take a well-earned break—from my work, at least." He smiled wryly.

"No problem," said Claire, raising her glass to Max and giving him a full on, wide eyed, teeth gleaming smile, which I thought was quite strange. She turned to Stuart. "It will be a pleasure working for you, Stuart."

I eyed Claire warily. She seemed different since her return from London, more brittle and edgy. Her appearance was different too. Her hair, which had been fairly short and a nondescript brown the last time I'd seen her, was now long, well past her shoulders, and highlighted very blonde. Her figure had become lean and lithe since she'd taken up running and going to the gym—at my suggestion, and I had barely started yet. What a joke. —and her skin, which I assumed was meant to be sun kissed, looked more like a chewed up caramel toffee.

Even her dress sense had changed; at one time she would never have worn such a short skirt and low-necked top together. I felt positively old fashioned and dowdy in my skinny jeans and long-sleeved shirt, which until now I had thought the height of fashion. I hoped upon hope that she didn't dress that way in the baker's shop.

In fact, I thought, with a frisson of shock. *She looks just like one of Max's girlfriends. Like a Barbie.*

To hide my alarm I gazed at my surroundings, at the gleaming cozy bar, all the seats filled with chattering diners. The pub was old, really old, dating back to the sixteenth century; in fact, only a little later than the life time of Margaret and Ursula Pole. It had a cozy thatched roof, and thick beams covered the ceilings. A wood burning stove glowed brightly in the huge fireplace, sending out a smoky, woody smell which I sniffed appreciatively.

"A penny for them, Hannah?" asked Max suddenly.

I was very conscious of the fact that I was sitting very close to him on the bench, our thighs almost touching. I was also very aware of how much he looked like Gregory, Gregory Walsh, who I hadn't seen for what seemed like ages—years, in fact. Or, of course, centuries.

"Oh," I said airily. "I was just thinking about this pub and how old it is. Also, did you know that there was a fire in Havant in seventeen sixty, which almost wiped out the whole town? The only buildings to survive were this pub and part of the church next door." I pointed in the general direction of St. Faith's Church. "Well, this pub was a row of cottages then."

"Really?" Max asked, as he took his eyes away from the menu—a large leather coated affair more like a book than a menu—to look at me. I noticed that a black clad waitress hovered uncertainly in the background. "You're very knowledgeable," he grinned, turning towards me. "A bit of an historian, are you?"

Before I could reply, Claire butted in. "Wow. A fire? You're making boring old Havant sound as exciting as London. You know, the fire in Pudding Lane and all that."

"Hey, don't knock Havant," I said. "We've got loads of claims to fame." I then went on to tell them about Warblington Manor and Margaret Pole and Henry the Eighth. As I got into it, I realized that I loved talking about them, and that in fact I was getting an almost perverse pleasure out of just saying their names.

Piped music played softly, and amidst the hubbub of the other diners—the pub was very busy as it was a Friday night—Stuart suggested that hadn't we better order our food. He nodded towards the waitress, who had moved slightly nearer and was clutching a note pad and pencil close to her chest like a shield.

We fell silent as we ordered our food, and then as Stuart and Claire carried on their conversation, Max turned towards me again and said very quietly, "Hannah, I think I need to make an apology about the other night."

I frowned, pretending that I didn't know what he was talking about.

"You know, in the cemetery. I don't really know what happened."

Slightly put out by his words, I replied, "Yeah, okay. I

39

know it was a mistake. There's no way you'd ever want to kiss me." *Oh my God, why did I say that?*

"Um...." Max fumbled for what to say. "Boss and personal assistant, Hannah? Not a good idea."

"You don't like me anyway," I pouted. *Oh my God, why did I say that?* The wine must have gone to my head. Stupidly I picked up my glass and took another deep slug. "I'm not your type," I hissed as that hot sweaty night club suddenly came to mind. There'd certainly been no kisses then.

Max opened his mouth to speak, and just about managed to utter, "That's not true—" when Claire, picking up on the venomous undertone between me and Max, gave a pointed glance while tossing her long blonde hair over her shoulder. Then, thank God, with such perfect timing, the waitress arrived with the food.

We ate with relish. The food was excellent, aromatic, and appetizing, taking the edge off the fact that I had maybe drank my wine a little too fast. I felt a bit fuzzy and out of control. I chatted with Stuart, noticing all the time that, from her seat opposite him, Claire flirted unashamedly with Max, frequently shaking her long blonde hair back from her face, giving the mega-watt smile, and even offering him tiny portions of food, which he ate from the tip of her fork in what I thought was a blatantly sexual way

Feeling more and more put out, and not really knowing why—why should I feel that way about Claire and Max? —I excused myself to Stuart, wondering if the other two would even notice that I'd gone, and went to the ladies' room. For once there was no queue and I went straight into a cubicle, still inwardly fuming at Claire's behavior with Max and wondering what it was all about.

Yeah, okay, Max's interest had obviously been ignited by

the fact that Claire now looked like a Barbie doll. But Claire's interest in Max? She'd never been attracted to him before. In fact, she'd always said that she didn't even like him, and I remembered her saying only recently that she thought he was up himself.

I gazed at myself in the mirror and shook my head sadly, seeing once again Max's gaze slipping from mine when I'd asked him what he'd been doing at the ruin that night. He was obviously hiding something. I was reluctant to go back to the bar with the others, afraid that I'd made a fool of myself and feeling pretty much left out of things, when I felt a gentle pulling at my arm and a face appeared at my side, making me catch my breath.

The face was virtually unlined, with smooth red cheeks surrounded by a fluted white bonnet tied under the chin. She was round and jolly as a Weeble, and wore a long skirt with a short sleeved embroidered peasant blouse tucked in, and a voluminous apron covered in very suspect rusty looking stains tied over the top. When she smiled, I noticed that some of her teeth were black as night.

"Come dear, come and lie down. I'm Mrs. Dawes, the midwife. You must stop pacing and come to the bed. The baby is coming."

She pulled at my arm again but not so gently this time, so that her nails, long and sharp as claws, dug into my skin. Glancing again into the mirror, I saw that its surface wavered brightly like a restless glassy sea, making my eyes feel tired and heavy until the lids, which I was valiantly trying to keep open, finally fell, and suddenly I, Hannah Palmer, was gone.

~*~

It was September, the ninth month, an ending month, yet the first month of the old Roman year. Even though it was early in the morning, barely seven o'clock, the sun hung like a golden disc, hot and heavy, spreading rapidly across a bright blue sky speckled with smoky tendrils of cloud. Its heat pierced the uneven glass of the windows, and spread around the room like thick yellow butter smeared on bread — over the walls, the floor, the ceiling, the wooden washstand, its flowered bowl and jug shiny and clean. It spread over the huge bed, its wooden headboard and footboard rising up like shields, and upon which I lay tangled in sweaty sheets that were clammy against my burning skin as I writhed and coiled in my bloody agony, my bloody pain.

Servants were scurrying around the bedchamber, hanging heavy tapestries at the windows to block out the light of the impending hot day, and lighting candles with long, smoldering tapers that now guttered fitfully on the bedside table and the shiny washstand. My pains had begun at the very first light, softly at first, gently, just a faint, irritating needling in the small of my back. Yet they woke me — the pains, and the birds, the noisy chattering, chirping birds that squawked and hustled and bustled in the blood red sky like a raucous party.

My mother, Margaret Pole, was there and I grabbed her hands. "Don't leave me, Mother," I begged her. "Don't leave me." The pains were bad now in my lower back, like nasty red-hot fingers pinching, and it felt as if a big man wearing hob nail boots was marching the length of my rigid spine, up and down, up and down. My huge stomach seemed to clench and unclench as I held it tightly with laced, white knuckled fingers. The baby was uncannily quiet, and very still.

"I will never leave you, Ursula, my Little Bear," my mother told me. "I will never leave you."

I was sitting now, my back against the headboard,

my legs wide open and the harsh cotton of my nightgown scraping over the bulging dome of my contracting stomach. The material felt wet and sticky against my breasts, which were full and leaking.

My mother was close to me. She held my hand tightly, securely, while the midwife, Mrs. Dawes, touched between my legs, her fingers prodding and poking, searching for the baby's tiny, furry head. The metallic odor of blood hung heavily as an abattoir in the hot air. I sat up higher and leaned forward, trying to bear down, to push hard. I knew I was grunting and squealing like an animal, like a pig rooting in mud and fallen leaves for truffles.

Time passed—endless time—and I opened my eyes. The room seemed even darker now, and from the gaps in the hangings, I saw the sun sinking into the earth like a fiery crimson ball. My mother's face floated in front of me like a pink puffy balloon. Her mouth was opening and closing, opening and closing. She spoke to me, but I couldn't hear what she was saying. Defeated, I closed my eyes.

"The shoulders—oh my God, the shoulders," said a voice—I thought it was Mrs. Dawes, the midwife. "I've got the head—I'm holding the head. She must push."

"She can't push anymore," my mother said tiredly. "Surely—not anymore."

The room was dark now, but I could see my mother pacing and pacing, then peering between the hangings, where blackness stood hard at the windows. Long deep shadows lurked in every corner. Candles guttered fitfully on the bedside table, a tiny flickering blue flame encased with gold. They smelled warm and greasy. I wanted to be sick. My mother held me securely, her arms around my stiff shoulders, as I retched and heaved.

43

"We're almost there. Just another push — a tiny push," said Mrs. Dawes, the midwife, and then I heard my mother's voice, her familiar beloved voice, irritable now and afraid.

"We'll have to cut her. Here, go on — you're the midwife. Take the knife. For God's sake, woman, you'll have to do it. I can't — she's my daughter. I can't do it." She wiped her sweating forehead with the back of her hand.

Soft empty sobbing filled the air and the room. My mother was hunched over, her black dress tight against rounded shoulders and her hands covering her face. Yet Mrs. Dawes, the midwife, stood at the bedside, cradling a baby in her crimson splattered arms, a sleek, naked baby. It was a boy, for I saw his tiny penis waving erect. He opened his mouth, a deep black cavern, and bawled long and loud. My swollen breasts leaked a long stream of thin tepid milk.

It was strange now, for I found that I was not in my body, but floating somewhere near the ceiling. It was good to feel so light and free and not hampered with a body, a heavy unresisting body. Yet where was my body? Had I died? The sun was coming up and had appeared, a lemon globe hanging in the sky, for the candles had long since flickered and gone.

The birds were chattering and chirping again, squabbling and quarrelling. Did they never rest? I floated nearer and nearer to the bed — to the figure on the bed, the blood-soaked figure on the bed. My heart banged heavily, so very heavily against my ribs. I cupped my mouth and my nose with my hands, my eyes bulged, and I bit my knuckles to stifle a scream, as I realized it was me.

~*~

I was in bed when I came round. I felt as if I'd been gone for years, and was not sure of the day or the time, or indeed the year. All I knew was that I was in my bedroom at number forty Mitchell Road, Bedhampton, tucked securely between crisp white sheets. My duvet smelled reassuringly of the sweet scent of comfort, and there was a glass of water on the bedside cabinet. White curtains decorated with enormous blue flowers were pulled across the window, but it didn't quite meet in the middle, and I could see that it was raining, and that little drops rolled down the glass like tears on a mourning face.

I was overwhelmed by sadness, such a deep, deep sadness, and I wondered why I felt that way. All of a sudden, memories came crashing into my mind and I was Ursula again, and the baby was coming and the pain was intense. I put my hand to my stomach. Yet my stomach was flat, flat as the proverbial ironing board. There was no baby there now. I remembered the midwife, Mrs. Dawes, holding him, holding my baby, his tiny face peeking from the crook of her arm like a slice of cream cheese. I'd had no chance to hold him, to feel his smooth skin against mine, or to kiss the tip of his tiny upturned nose.

I rolled my head restlessly on the pillow and, as I tried to sit up to reach for the water, the aching in my body intensified and I felt bruised and sore, as if I'd been severely pummeled in a fight which I had definitely lost. I lay back down with a sigh.

There was a tiny tap on the door and Sarah, her eyes wide, poked her head into the room and said, "Hey, Hannah? Are you okay? Can I come in?"

"Yes Sarah, of course, come in." I beckoned with my head.

"Hey, you don't have to worry," she told me as she came to sit on the bed. "I'm past the infectious stage." When I must have looked puzzled, she added, "You know — the shingles."

"Oh yes," I said, but not really understanding or

45

remembering. With all that had happened to me, I'd forgotten about Sarah's shingles, but still asked her if she was feeling better.

She shrugged and said, "Hey, so so — maybe a bit."

Leaning towards me, she placed a hand on my forehead, which felt good, cool and reassuring. Then she playfully asked, "Hey, how are you feeling now? Are you hung over? You were really out of it last night." She looked at the bedside cabinet. "Do you want this water?"

Gratefully I took the glass from her as Sarah helped me to sit up and put a pillow against the headboard so that I could rest my back.

"How did I get home from the pub last night?" I asked her. "What day is it? Oh my God, Sarah, what happened?"

"Hey, Claire dropped you off in a taxi," she told me. "She said she'd found you collapsed in the toilet, and that you'd had too much to drink, as usual. And it's Saturday — luckily, no work for you today."

"As usual?" I asked, "What did she mean by that? I'm not usually drunk. I mean, it's not a regular thing, you know."

Sarah shrugged. "Hey I know, but that's what she said."

"Did I say anything last night?" I asked tentatively.

"Hey, um...not really. Well, you just kept holding your stomach and saying that you hurt. Oh, and that you wanted your mother. But I just assumed that you said that because you were drunk. For some strange reason people do want their mum's when they're in that state."

I smiled at her and nodded, and then, taking a sip of water, I asked her, "What about Max and Stuart?"

"Hey, they went home, I suppose," she said with a frown. "You don't need to worry about them, they'll have been fine. How come you collapsed in the toilets, Hannah? That's really not like you. And what's happened to Claire? She looks like one of Max's Barbie dolls."

I managed to grin at her as I nodded my head. "I know. I don't know how it happened, but yeah, you're right, she's become a Barbie. My sister is a Barbie doll. Oh no."

We giggled together, and Sarah patted my hand and began to stand up, saying, "Hey, oh well, I'd better leave you to it. Is there anything I can get you? Would you like something to eat?"

I shook my head wearily, feeling as if I'd been through hell and back and wondering where it was all going to end. I worried that if I was going to live Ursula Pole's life that I really would have to go through all fourteen pregnancies and, feeling as I did now after just one labor, that it could well be the death of me.

Before I knew what I was doing, I said, "Sarah, do you remember a few weeks ago when I talked to you about the strange experience that I'd had, and you told me about Margaret Pole and Warblington Manor and all that stuff?"

She nodded her head and sat down again, "Hey yes, I do. What's happened, Hannah?"

"This is going to be hard to understand, Sarah, but please just listen to me, will you?"

She nodded again and put her hand in mine as I began to speak. The rain, falling harder now from a metallic grey sky, drummed against the window, so I had to raise my voice for Sarah to hear.

"Sarah, I didn't collapse in the toilet. I wasn't really drunk — well, a little bit tipsy. I'd only had a couple of glasses of wine." I took a deep breath. "It might seem as if I'm hung over, but the truth of it is that I'm just completely worn out." I paused for a split second, then carried on. "I gave birth last night, to a baby boy. I had a really bad time. In fact, I'm not sure if I died temporarily. I definitely remember floating on the ceiling and looking down at my body."

"Hey, who were you?" she asked, with what seemed a genuine understanding and interest.

"I think that I was Ursula Pole and— Oh my God, Sarah, according to Wikipedia she gave birth to fourteen children."

I watched her face intently as I spoke, and to say her reaction to my story blew me away is a total understatement.

Chapter Five

The day was hot and humid, the sun a yellow ball in a deep blue sky baking the garden and muting the vibrant colors of the flower beds and the lawns. The scent of cornflowers and columbine hung in the air like a line of washing as I ran outside, my father's dogs, Gilbert and Sturdy, running ahead, barking with excitement as I threw them a shuttlecock and they raced to catch it.

I was happy, so happy, for no real reason other than that it was May and I was but fifteen years old and the day was bright and I wore a new gown of vibrant green silk, the long bell sleeves slashed to reveal the palest oyster pink to ever have been seen — or so I thought. I ran and jumped and danced across the lawns, my soft green slippers sliding across the grass as if on ice. I put my face to the sun and threw the shuttlecock again and the dogs, their tails wagging, ran again to fetch it to me.

My father, Sir Richard Pole, and my mother, Margaret Pole, her arm hung over his like a claw, sailed by on their walk, and my brothers, all four of them — Henry, Arthur, Reginald, and Geoffrey, swaggering like painted peacocks — took the air before dinner was to be served. They walked in crocodile two's, each of them with their hands behind their backs, their heads low and pointing forward, the colors of their suits even brighter and more vibrant than my own gown.

I danced along the paved pathway, and from there into the coolness of the overhanging branches of the trees, where lozenges of sunlight peeked between soft green leaves and spangled the dry ground. The sound of the dogs barking became fainter and fainter as they joined my father, my mother, and my brothers, the dog, Gilbert, holding the shuttlecock securely in his mouth, no doubt encouraging the others to play fetch now that I had escaped them.

Taking hold of my voluminous skirts with both hands, I swayed from side to side, taking great pleasure in the swishing of the silk against the soft material of my new lacy undergarments.

I stood still then, humming softly under my breath, raising my face again to the sun and reveling in the warmth on my tender young skin. I closed my eyes tightly, very tightly, the sun becoming a red angry mist behind them, and when I opened them, very, very slowly, he was standing there, as I knew he would be. I smiled coyly at him and he smiled back, tiny wrinkles around his eyes fanning out like the marks of the sea breaking on the sandy beach at Southsea.

"My lady." He bowed deeply from the waist, lowering his eyes and then, because he could wait no longer, looked up and grinned as cheekily as a little boy.

"Arise, Sir Gregory," I demanded imperiously, waving my arm with a flourish.

With a smile, he took me into the warm circle of his arms and I melted into his long lean body as his mouth sought mine. We kissed, our tongues entwined and his mouth warm and wet, when all of a sudden the sound of a fanfare rang throughout the hot still air, and Gregory and I, drawing slightly apart, stared at each other in disbelief, both thinking the same thing.

"Was that the king's fanfare?"

But then all became quiet, all became still, and, thinking it had been our imagination, we relaxed again. I buried my face in the curve of his neck to feel his pulse beat rapidly beneath my lips.

The excited barking of Gilbert and Sturdy alerted us once more, and pandemonium ensued as my mother, closely followed by my father and my brothers, sped past as if chased by the hounds of hell.

"Henry," I heard my mother say. "Oh my goodness, Henry—he is here."

They didn't see Gregory and I in our secret hiding place amongst the trees, and probably wouldn't have seen us anyway being in such a panic at the king's unannounced arrival.

The king's fanfare sounded again, louder and closer now, and a creaking like old arthritic joints was heard as the drawbridge slowly raised and horses, their hooves pounding, cantered through, followed by the marching of boots. At the head of the procession, the royal standard fluttered in the breeze as King Henry the Eighth of England and his retinue thundered into the gardens of Warblington Manor, the royal carriage rocking dangerously from side to side. Frantic neighing shrieked through the air. Gregory, with one last frantic look at me, fled away, while I ran across the gardens in pursuit of my family.

Such was his height he had to stoop as he came through the great door into the shadowy hallway of our home, clutching his cloak around him which, although travel stained, was sumptuous and rich. My mother bowed so low that her nose touched the aromatic rushes that were strewn over the flagged floor.

"Arise, my Margaret, my kin," boomed Henry, reminding me of what I had said earlier to Gregory when he had bowed in front of me.

He stood with his large meaty hands on his hips, legs wide open and feet planted like a sturdy tree. Sunshine streamed through the tiny windows, gilding his blond hair that stood around his head like a halo. He was a handsome man, with eyes of bright blue and full round cheeks sprinkled with faint stubble. Dressed richly in a cloth of gold, pure white feathers adorned his hat and rings sparkled on his fingers. His codpiece, decorated with diamonds and pearls, stood out proudly.

"Feed me and water me, my kin Margaret, for my stomach is empty and my throat parched." Behind him his men stood to attention, their swords hanging like silver rods from their waists, dirt and sweat seeming to ooze from their pores like a fast flowing river.

All of a sudden, his gaze fell on me. Narrowing his eyes and squatting to my height, his powerful thighs folding beneath him, he said, "Ah, Ursula...belle Ursula. You are grown." He glanced up at my mother and father with his hot blue eyes. "I have a husband for this one." And when my mother looked just a little afraid, he said, "Just you wait and see."

A shiver ran down my spine.

"It is so good to see you, Henry," said my mother, able, it seemed, to find her voice at last. "Your visit is such a lovely surprise. But come, follow me, for there is food and drink within."

Drawing himself up tall and strong, towering over us

like a giant from a story book, Henry stood at his full height, surveying us all.

~*~

The ringing of my mobile brought me back this time, and a beep as a text message came through. Groggily I lifted my head from where it had been resting on the hard, wooden desk, and I cautiously rolled my neck to ease the stiffness. My computer screen was blank, but as I knocked against the mouse it sprang to life, showing that the last thing I had been looking at was the emails in my Hotmail account. Vague noises sounded around the building, and I could hear Claire typing in next door's office.

Picking up my mobile, I put it to my ear and said, "Hello?"

"Hannah, are you okay?"

"Oh, hi Mum. Yes, fine. You?"

"I can't stay to chat," she said. "And I know you're busy too. I just wanted to remind you about tea tonight. Come around between five and six?"

"Yes, of course," I told her. "See you tonight, Mum." Gratefully I hung up and put my mobile back on the desk beside me. *Thank God*, I thought, *that she didn't want a long conversation. I wouldn't be capable of that — not after the trauma of meeting King Henry.* I looked around, half expecting him to appear in the office and look at me with those piercing blue eyes, that sneering gaze. Once again a shiver ran down my spine, and I understood fully then why I had such a cruel husband, knowing now that he had been chosen for me by the king.

Remembering the text that had come through as I woke up, I reached for my phone again, surprised that the text wasn't from Gregory, but from Claire, also reminding me of tonight's tea, and that we could go together after work. She obviously thought it was funny to send me a text from the office next door instead of coming to speak to me. *Oh, ha ha, Claire.*

I didn't know why, but I became frantic then, searching through my texts, desperate to read one from Gregory to be assured of his presence and confirm when we could meet again. I found messages from Sarah, more from Claire, a few from Mum, even texts from my ex Andy and Max and Stuart, but nothing from Gregory. I scrolled through my contacts, becoming increasingly distraught when I couldn't find any trace of him. *Gregory,* I thought. *What's happened to Gregory?*

It hit me suddenly like a ton of bricks, the realization that Gregory didn't have a mobile phone, that he had lived a long time ago before text messages and phone calls existed, and that there was no way he would be in my contacts for that reason alone. Tears poured down my face. I sniffed and rubbed my eyes wearily with the pads of my fingers.

Glancing out of the window, I saw that the sky was a pale blue dotted with creamy clouds, and the sun shone, yet tiny spots of rain pattered at the window and dotted the moist earth around the daffodils and tulips with tiny holes. A slight wind blew, causing the flowers to bend and sway in their pots.

I was dabbing at my face with a screwed up tissue when Max walked into the office carrying a tottering pile of buff colored folders, which he put down heavily on the desk before he realized I was there. He looked taken aback when he saw me, and said, "Oh Hannah, you're here. Sorry about these." He pointed to the folders. "I was hoping that you could file them away for me."

"Yes, of course," I replied.

"Anything wrong?" he asked, standing in front of me, his hands on his hips, much like Henry's stance — typical male, although thank God no codpiece anywhere in sight. He looked so worried, so concerned, that I almost burst into tears again, so tempted to tell him everything, to pour out my heart, so to speak. I was just about to do that and Max had opened his mouth to speak when Claire walked into the office and his attention was immediately diverted by her Barbie like presence.

Her appearance for work dismayed me, and I did a double take thinking that maybe I'd entered another parallel universe, and had found myself in a night club in the nineteen sixties or seventies. She wore a skirt so short that it resembled a very thick belt. Her long slim legs were encased in black opaque tights, and she tottered in sky high heels. Her top, either made for a child or shrunk in a very hot wash, clung to her slim waist, and her breasts peeked out of the low neck like two huge bouncy balls. Had she had a boob job? I didn't know about my eyes, but Max's bore a startling resemblance to an extremely surprised frog.

"Oh, you're here, are you?" she said, looking at me but taking no notice whatsoever of Max, which I thought was quite rude.

"Of course I am."

"Where have you been?"

"Nowhere," I replied, frowning, shaking my head. "Here?"

"No, I don't think you have," said Max suddenly, obviously having gotten over his initial reaction to Claire's appearance and able to speak. "I was just about to ask you where you'd been."

"Yeah," butted in Claire. "Why do you think I sent you a text about tea at Mum's tonight instead of just speaking to you? You weren't here, Hannah."

"Oh, I just thought you were being silly," I giggled. "Or maybe being lazy—you know, not wanting to actually walk into this office from that office." I pointed in the vague direction of where Claire had come from.

Claire said nothing, just stood there staring at me, her arms folded over the enormous globes that stuck out on her chest.

Max, perching on the edge of the desk now, said, "Look, Hannah, if you ever do need to pop out, to go to the shop or whatever, please let me know first, will you? I was worried—it's not like you to just disappear."

"Yeah," butted in Claire. "Particularly as your mobile was left on the desk. You don't usually like being parted from your precious phone."

I opened my mouth to speak, but thought, *Why bother? They won't believe me if I tell them where I have been, so it's best to say nothing at all.* I was puzzled, though, because I'd always thought that my physical presence remained here in this time when I was back in the 1500s. After all, Claire had found me supposedly drunk in the ladies' room when I was gone the last time. *Hmm*, I thought. *Very strange.*

While I'd been busy thinking, Max and Claire had disappeared. I'd vaguely heard her asking for a document that she needed for her work, and apparently Stuart had told her it was in Max's office. I could hear the rumble of Max's voice, and Claire's high-pitched giggles as they walked—well, Claire wiggled—across the spacious entrance area and into the office. The door closed with a click.

I felt like a naughty school girl that had been told off by her parents. Really, what did it matter to either of them if I was there or not? Why was Max so worried? Where on earth did he think I was? Feeling naughtier than ever, I tiptoed across the tiled entrance way and stopped at Max's office, where I pressed my ear against the sturdy wooden door. Grinning, a vague memory of my mum being nosy and listening in to our next-door neighbors came to mind. I recalled her shushing me, a finger to her lips, and putting her ear to a glass pressed against the wall.

Hmm, I thought. *I could try that.*

But before I could go to the kitchen to get one of our many glasses, I heard Max's rumbling voice again, followed by jovial laughter, and then another higher pitched voice chimed in. Very much put out now by Max and Claire's behavior — it just wasn't professional — I began very slowly to turn the brass knob and, as I did so, the door began to open, a tiny sliver at a time.

Putting a narrowed eye to the crack, I peered through, but the room was very dark, strangely dark, and something was flickering. Was it candles, or were the bulbs failing? Why would Max have candles in his office? To set a romantic scene for him and Claire? Totally ridiculous.

Glancing behind me, I saw that the entrance way was now almost pitch black, and dark creepy shadows lurked in every corner. As my eyes adjusted to the light, a massive fireplace set deep into one thick wall came into view, along with a wooden settle with a high back and arms, and a gleaming sideboard, chunky tallow candles standing on its top.

The area looked more like an ante-chamber than an entrance hall now. Alarm bells began to ring, and the realization that I was Ursula Pole again crashed into my mind. With no holding back because of that, I flung the door wide open to find that it wasn't an office now, but a bedchamber, and the flickering that I'd seen was indeed from candles covering, it seemed, every surface.

The couple laying on the bed entwined in each other's arms turned languidly towards me, their faces drugged with desire. Without any feelings of shock or surprise whatsoever, I saw that it was my husband, Henry Stafford, and William Palmer, a very talented musician in the court of King Henry the Eighth of England.

Chapter Six

I told Max that I wasn't feeling good, and asked if he would mind very much if I went home when I poked my head around the door of what was once again Max's office. It was no longer a bedchamber, where my husband, many centuries before, had been committing adultery not with a woman, as I had half expected, but a man—and a man well known at court, too. I knew that William Palmer was a new boy on the block, so to speak, and a favorite of Henry the King as well as my husband Henry. Well, his particular favorite, it seemed.

I didn't know what I expected when I peered into Max's office, but there seemed to be a sudden shifting in my vision, as if they'd quickly drawn apart. But when I looked again the two of them were sitting quite properly, Max at his desk and Claire in what was usually my chair, searching through documents that looked so yellow and old, even ancient, I was surprised that they didn't crumble to dust in their fingers. Claire, the belt that she wore masquerading as a skirt and showing all of her legs, was handling them very carefully, almost reverently, I thought.

I narrowed my eyes suspiciously, but thought that perhaps it was the effect of my going back in time so recently and the nature of what I had seen that had made me see something that wasn't there. And really, I didn't think that Max would act in such an unprofessional way in his own offices. After all, there was a time and a place for everything.

All the same, I couldn't help but feel a pang of jealousy as I watched the two of them sitting so companionably together; so happily, it seemed. *It should be me*, I thought. *Me and Max. I am his super-efficient personal assistant, not Claire.* I wanted to stamp my feet and pout like a child, but with some sort of super human strength I managed to restrain myself.

Max stood up and walked towards me, his expression concerned. He laid a hand on my shoulder. "Of course, Hannah, have the afternoon and see how you feel tomorrow. I hope you haven't caught Sarah's shingles—you do live with her—and, well, Hannah…." He hesitated before speaking again. "Maybe you need to see a doctor? Um…or speak to somebody, a counsellor?"

Claire, frowning, looked taken aback.

"No," I shook my head. "Sarah only said the other day that she's not contagious any more. I don't think it's that. I just feel really tired, and I've got a sore throat and headache. I'll be fine for tomorrow. And, no, I don't think I need a doctor, or a counsellor. What makes you think that, Max?"

"Oh, I don't know. You seem troubled lately. Forget it, Hannah, I'm sorry." He sat down again, and I noticed that he was blushing. The "I'm so great" Max Reynolds blushing? Well, that was a turn up for the books.

"Are you still coming to Mum's tonight?" asked Claire suspiciously.

I nodded my head. "I hope so. If I still feel off it later, though, I'll text you."

I drove home, my hands still shaky on the wheel. It seemed

that all this going backwards and forwards in time was taking its toll. Tears came into my eyes again, obscuring my vision. Frantically I blinked them away, trying to concentrate on the road and wondering where it would all end.

Sarah, I thought. *I need to speak to Sarah.*

Thinking about what she had confided to me the other day—her shocking confession, so to speak, about her own experiences of going back in time—I knew without a doubt that she was the only person who would understand what I was going through."

She was in the sitting room when I arrived home, curled up on the settee reading a book. Even though she'd been ill, she still looked well groomed, very neatly dressed, and her hair was styled in its usual gleaming bob. She jumped up when she saw me, and looking at my face seemed to know everything. After helping me with my coat, she led me to an armchair and gently sat me down. Oh, how good it was to be home.

She then disappeared into the kitchen, where very soon I heard the kettle bubbling to the boil and the clink of mugs and spoons. After handing me a large mug of hot coffee—laced with whiskey, I thought, as I sniffed at the steaming brew—she sat down again and said, "Hey, okay, Hannah, what's happened?"

As I filled her in on my latest time travel experience, I felt as though I was telling her about an episode in a soap opera that was watched by millions on the telly, like *Coronation Street* or *Eastenders*. I supposed in this case it could be called *Medieval Avenue* or *Henry's Way*, for he certainly did seem to have had his own way most of the time. Her eyes widened when I told her about my meeting with King Henry, and widened even further when I described the very brief experience I'd had when seeing my husband, Henry Stafford, in a very compromising position with a male musician from King Henry's court.

She blew carefully on her drink and took a tentative sip, saying, "Hey, maybe it's time for you to see someone, Hannah. A counsellor?"

I looked at her in disbelief. "That's exactly what Max said earlier. But I'm not sure...."

"Hey, I went to a woman who did past life regression," she told me.

"What's the point of that? Don't you, just as I do, go back spontaneously? Why would we need anybody to do it for us?"

"Hey, it helped me to talk to somebody who was aware of this type of thing. I felt at one point that I was going mad."

I smiled at her. "Yes, I feel that way too. And I long to see Gregory, even though I know that maybe he doesn't even exist." I glanced at her as I spoke, and then said quietly, "Do you know something, Sarah? Gregory looks just like Max."

"Hey, Max?" she said, startled. "Our Max? Max Reynolds?"

I nodded. "Yeah, and I get confused between them sometimes, and...." I couldn't help giggling, with nerves I supposed. "I'm in love with Gregory, so it sort of feels as if I'm in love with Max too. When I'm not, of course. It's really weird."

"Hey, that must be really strange," she replied thoughtfully, sipping from her mug. "Hmm, you'll have to try to detach yourself, Hannah." She looked straight at me. "I didn't really think you had much time for Max, though."

"Well...," I stammered, "I like him as a boss. But he's...." My voice trailed away, and for once I was lost for words, so instead of speaking I took a huge gulp of coffee, almost choking on the hot brew.

"Hey, Hannah, have you been a bit jealous since Claire came along looking like one of Max's Barbies?"

I didn't want to say it—I didn't want anybody to even know it. But I nodded and said, "Yes, unfortunately I have."

"Hey, just you wait and see," Sarah said. "Max will end up with a girl that doesn't resemble a Barbie at all—and that could well be you."

"Oh God no," I replied, laughing manically. "I'm not that jealous." There was a short silence between us, which I filled by saying, "I'm grateful to have you to talk to, Sarah. Apart from the lady who did past life regression, did you have anybody else to confide in?"

Sarah shook her head, just a tiny bit too quickly for my liking, as she said, "Hey, no—nobody at all." Abruptly, she stood up and went to the sideboard, where she fumbled around in one of the drawers and then sat back down again, handing me a small yellow business card with the name Sonia Fewer, Counsellor and Past Life Specialist, printed across it in spiky black letters.

"Hey, just in case?" she said.

I nodded and thanked her, and then told her what Claire and Max had said to me earlier; that I hadn't been in the office all morning, and that they were wondering where I was. It seemed as if my physical presence had gone from this time and was in the other world, and that didn't usually happen.

Sarah shrugged and said, "Hey, you're right, that is unusual. I'm not sure why it happens. Were you with Gregory at that time?"

"Yes, for some of it. But then I met Henry, the king."

"Hey, perhaps subconsciously you want to actually stay

63

there with Gregory because you're in love with him. Love is powerful, Hannah, really powerful."

I nodded. "Yeah, I can see that. Yes, I want to stay with Gregory, but I certainly haven't any desire to stay back there with the king. I don't trust him. He was really nice to my mother, Margaret Pole, when he turned up at Warblington Manor unannounced, but look at what he eventually did to her."

Sarah smiled wryly and said, "Hey, yeah, he was an evil one, was that Henry. Whatever, though, I think being in love with Gregory has a huge bearing on whether or not you take your physical body with you or leave it here."

I felt so much better; my headache and sore throat had miraculously disappeared as if I'd never been ill at all. Maybe it was the whiskey that Sarah had put in my coffee, or perhaps just the fact that I'd had somebody to talk to who understood. I wasn't sure what it was, but it was good to be well and, glancing at my watch — a very disappointing 1,250 steps today — I saw with relief that I had plenty of time before I was due for tea at Mum and Dad's.

I stood up and peered from the window. The day had brightened considerably and the rain had stopped, and although there were dirty swollen clouds floating up there amongst the blue, I still wanted to get out of the house. "Do you fancy a walk, Sarah?" I asked. "I thought maybe I might have a trip out to Warblington Cemetery again. I'll drive — "

"Hey, Hannah, that's perhaps not a good idea. You might find yourself going back again. And, no, thanks, I'm still not totally okay. I think I'll stay here and get back to my book. And, anyway, Neil might be calling round later."

Shrugging on my coat, I said, "Okay, say hi to Neil." Then I shook my head. "No, I've already been back twice today; I don't think it will happen again."

"Hey, no worries, Hannah. I've enjoyed our chat, but be careful, okay?"

"I will. I'm going to Mum and Dad's for tea, so won't be back until later."

She nodded and I turned to leave, but there was just one last issue that I wanted to resolve before I did. I turned back. "Sarah?" She looked up from her book, a questioning look on her face. "I didn't like to ask before, and you've never volunteered the information, but I have to know." I took a deep breath. "Who were you when you went back?"

Sarah stared at me for what seemed an eternity, but eventually said, with no hey to precede it this time — it wasn't really needed. "Elizabeth the First, Queen of England."

~*~

I walked briskly amongst the gravestones in Warblington Cemetery. I hadn't gone to the ruin yet, and I wasn't sure if I was going to today. As Sarah had said, I was running the risk of going back, and I didn't really think I could cope with it again today, especially as I was seeing Mum and Dad soon — and Claire, the all-knowing, all seeing sister, and also my little brother, Ryan. Even so, my mind was still spinning with the information that Sarah had given me.

Elizabeth the First, Queen of England, Henry's daughter with Anne Boleyn — wow. Imagine living her life. My life as Ursula Pole seemed quite mediocre compared to that. But of course, Elizabeth didn't have the trauma of pregnancies and births as poor Ursula had. And that must never be forgotten.

I found it intriguing that Ursula's eldest daughter, Dorothy, was a very influential lady at Elizabeth's court at the time of Ursula's death at the grand old age of sixty-six. After so many childbirths, I had been totally gob smacked to read that Ursula had lived to such a ripe old age, life expectancy not being anything near as long as it was today. There were so many deaths during childbirth in those times. She was certainly one brave woman. Hey — as Sarah would say — thank you, Dorothy, for being the link between mine and Sarah's past life experiences, and you're definitely not the weakest link. Haha, how funny was I?

Being so totally wrapped up in my thoughts, I failed to notice that the grey clouds from earlier had turned heavy and black and, swollen as cow's udders waiting to be milked, looked fit to burst, which suddenly they did. As the first drops fell, I ran quickly into the old cemetery of St. Thomas à Becket and took shelter beneath the wide spreading branches of the ancient yew tree.

Even though rain drummed through the branches and slid like little teardrops down the bright green leaves, I remained warm and dry, as if I was in my own little house, my own den, just like the grass dens that Claire and I used to make at the park when we were little girls. The salty smell of the sea was all around, clean and invigorating. I put my gloved hands deep into the pockets of my coat and, pulling my hood over my head, just stood there waiting for the rain to stop.

Glancing around, I noticed that I was surrounded by very old leaning gravestones, some black as coal like rotting teeth in a peasant's mouth, just like Mrs. Dawes the midwife. I wandered from one to the other, still managing to keep dry beneath the branches of the tree, the span was so wide. Most of the stones were hard to read, the wording being faded, and on some of them almost gone completely. But one stood out from among the rest, having fairly legible writing on it if I peered really closely.

My heart skipped a beat as I saw the name of Walsh clearly

etched in capital letters on its surface. On brushing away the ivy and furry moss that had grown all over it, I saw that the stone was heart shaped. Frantically I pulled away more and more of the plant, my nails breaking as I tried to dislodge it from the roots that clung stubbornly like little white worms deep into the earth. My hands became streaked with dust and dirt as I rubbed at the stone's grimy surface, until as if by magic the following words were revealed to me:

WALSH
Beneath this stone lies the mortal remains of
Eliza Walsh
Aged 32 years at the time of her death
Most beloved wife of Isaac Walsh and
Most cherished mother of Gregory and Alice
May the Angels guide her home

Thinking that my heart would burst with grief for Eliza, who surely must be Gregory's mother, but reassured that Gregory had existed and that I, as Ursula Pole, had loved him truly and deeply, I sank to my knees and there in the dusty, sweet smelling rain soaked earth put my hands to my face and wept.

Chapter Seven

I awoke feeling vulnerable and confused, my first thought being, "Where am I?" and even "Who am I, Hannah or Ursula?" Sitting up and gazing around, I saw with relief that I was Hannah and I was in bed at home, in the house that I shared with Sarah, the house that we had bought together.

Heaving a great sigh, I lay back down and closed my eyes, feeling an overwhelming temptation to snuggle down beneath the duvet and go back to sleep. But a working day awaited me and, because I'd had the previous afternoon off sick, I had a lot to do and didn't really want to let Max down. Thoughts of that afternoon came into my mind, and I smiled as I recalled the cemetery at St. Thomas à Becket Church and the ancient gravestone that I had found. How lucky I had been to find that one special gravestone amongst so many.

I recalled the strange flashback that I'd had when being with Gregory for the first time. I'd known somehow that his mother had died and that she lay beneath a heart shaped stone in Warblington Cemetery. Frowning and shaking my head, I mulled over how I'd known that. It was strange, but I just had.

"Gregory," I said proudly. "I have found your mother's

grave." I felt a strange aching in my breast every time I thought of her, poor Eliza, and poor Isaac, her husband. He must have missed her so much—even the wording on her stone showed how much they'd all cared for her. She was too young to die, only thirty-two, and surely he must have been of a similar age.

I was curious as to what had happened to him, whether he had remarried or had more children. Who knew? I didn't think Google would give me any further information. I couldn't find Gregory, let alone Eliza or Isaac. And now Alice had come into the picture, Gregory's sister. I vowed that next time I went back, I would ask Gregory about her.

Stretching and rousing myself, I noticed that warm sunshine poured in a narrow band through the opening in the curtains, making the room feel stuffy and airless. Clambering out of bed, I opened a window to let in some air, and peered from the window at the sky arching overhead, washed pale blue from yesterday's rain.

The garden, totally unkempt when we'd moved in, was finally taking shape, the lawns looking smooth and green and the flower beds weed free and vibrant with the yellows and oranges of daffodils and tulips. Sarah and I had been really pleased to find that we were now not only the proud owners of a lovely three-bedroom house and a big garden, but a pond teeming with goldfish and an overhanging weeping willow tree, its long skinny branches skimming the surface of the water.

The previous owners must have kept budgies, for a large wooden aviary stood close to the pond; empty now, of course, expect for stray fluffy feathers in pale blue and green that littered the ground, along with tiny seeds and bits of cuttlebone. The proverbial shed stood right at the bottom of the garden, and then the allotment for which Sarah and I had great plans for growing our own vegetables. "Hey," as Sarah would say, "We're going to be living off the land."

A voice sounded at my side and I turned my head, but there was nobody there and the voice, a man's voice, was obviously too deep to be Sarah's. What would Sarah be doing in my room anyway? Had the voice said something about Henry? Was I imagining things? Or, and this was quite scary, was I on the verge of taking a trip back in time? A fleeting picture of Ursula lying as if she were dead on her birthing bed flashed into my mind. I knew that Ursula hadn't died at that time, so I was desperate to know what had happened to her, and especially to the baby.

Taking a deep breath, I tried to concentrate on what I needed to do to get ready for work. I gathered together toiletries for the shower, then went to the large walk-in cupboard that I used as a wardrobe. Two of the great things that I liked about 1950s houses was that there was always a large garden and plenty of storage space.

Stepping into the cupboard, I remembered what it had looked like when we had first moved in—just a big, black, cavernous space, dark and dirty, festooned with spider's webs, and weirdly, a poster of a pop star from the 1960s hidden right at the back. "Hey, that's Cliff Richard," I remembered Sarah saying. "Hey, somebody obviously had a crush on him."

"Some crush. Why hide the poor man right at the back of a dark cupboard?"

She'd shrugged and I'd laughed, and we'd thrown the poster in the bin and carried on with our renovations, and the cupboard was now a very swish walk-in wardrobe. Flicking through my clothes, all hung neatly in rows, I pulled out a pair of smart black trousers and a black and white top with loose bell sleeves, which teamed with a red jacket and one or two pieces of jewelry would look good for the office.

Looking through my clothes brought Claire to mind, and the inappropriate things that she'd been wearing lately. Even my family had made the odd pointed remark at tea last night when they saw what Claire had worn to work that day. Poor Dad had blushed as red as his greenhouse tomatoes when she appeared at the tea table wearing a tight low-necked top, her breasts rising out of the top like two suet dumplings.

"What's going on?" asked Ryan, in a stage whisper that everybody could hear, including Claire, his cheeky teenage face creased in a grin. "Claire looks like that doll now, doesn't she? What's she called?" And when no one replied, he nudged Dad. "You know who I mean." Dad almost choked on his broccoli while Mum, a smile tugging at her lips, kept unusually quiet.

My wardrobe also brought to mind Ursula's first-born daughter, Dorothy, who had served as mistress of the robes to Queen Elizabeth the First. I shook my head in wonder at the thought that dealing with my clothes would be no problem for her after looking after Queen Elizabeth's no doubt vast array of beautiful gowns.

I heard a voice close to me again, and then a tiny tap on the door brought me out of my reverie. Assuming it was Sarah, as I knew that Neil hadn't stayed over and there was nobody else in the house, I called out, "Come in Sarah." Silence, a deep dark silence. I glanced at the door, fully expecting it to open, and when it didn't I walked towards it, saying, "Sarah? Sarah?"

I pulled the door open and a man walked in holding a crying baby, a man that I had seen so recently entwined in the arms of another man. He was dressed richly for the time in a short, embroidered smock pleated at the neck and wrists, his spindly legs covered in a thick hose that nowadays would be called thermal underwear.

Taking in the whole appearance of my husband, for this must surely be Henry Stafford, his long straggly hair receding so far at the hairline that half his head was bald, and glassy bulging fish eyes, I could definitely see that he was no Gregory — or Max.

"Ursula, darling, I've brought Henry to see you. He's been crying for his mother. Even his moppet has not stopped his tears." He showed me a tiny cloth doll with a round face and cheeks as red as berries.

Glancing down at myself, I saw that I no longer wore my favorite Betty Boop pajamas, but a gown, a night gown, edged in creamy lace and pink bows. I was in a sumptuous bedchamber, the wooden floor beneath my bare feet strewn with sweet smelling herbs, and the bed messy and unmade as if I'd just gotten up. A fire burned sulkily in the grate, and smoke, grey as ash, belched into the room. A wooden rocking crib stood at the bedside, and it was into this that Henry, my husband, placed the baby who, red faced, cried even louder, twisting and turning his small body in the tight swaddling clothes.

A servant came in carrying a breakfast tray of bread and spicy ale, which she placed on the bedside table. Then, after catching sight of Henry, she bobbed me a hasty curtsy and scurried out. Gently picking up the baby, I sat down on the nursing chair and, cradling his head in my palm, rocked him gently against my shoulder. His cries stopped immediately as he snuggled, whimpering, into my neck.

"Ssh, little Henry, ssh little Henry," I crooned, breathing in deeply the milky scent of his skin, his warm skin — in fact, his very warm skin. As I put a hand to little Henry's burning forehead, I felt a tiny pinprick of fear shoot along my spine, for there were rumors of smallpox in the village.

Also, I felt strange and disorientated because I didn't know where I was. I wasn't in the bedchamber where I had given birth to baby Henry, so I wasn't in Warblington Manor. Unless, of course, I had been in this house but in a different room, a separate room that was used for lying in. I very much doubted that Henry would have allowed me to stay at my mother's house to have our baby. I wasn't sure, but I got the impression that there was little love between them.

"Where is my mother?" I asked.

Henry, pacing backwards and forwards across the room, his hands laced together behind his back, suddenly stopped still and, glaring at me, said sarcastically, "Your mother, Ursula? Why, my dear one, your mother is obviously at home in her own house, where she belongs. You spend far too much time wanting to be with your mother. You have your own household now, your own husband and child. You must grow used to that."

I swallowed hastily seeing the glint in his eyes, the murderous glint in his eyes. I'd seen that look only once before, and that on the day that he'd struck me. But he had vowed never to do that again, and I would hold him to that, particularly not in the presence of our son.

"I only wondered, dear husband. She is my mother." I felt a sudden pang at the thought of my mother being so far away in Warblington. It could take days or even weeks to get to her. And Gregory too; how would I be able see him if I was so far away.

Glancing at Henry and the harshness of his unforgiving face, I dreaded what he would do if he ever found out about my love affair with, what would be to him, the lowly gardener, Gregory Walsh.

"Wondering, dear Ursula, is for fools," he said, coming so close that I could feel the spit from his not so fresh breath on my face. "You should be grateful that you are kept here in this sumptuous house by my family. By my father, the duke of Buckingham—a powerful man, Ursula, a very powerful man. A close confidante to the king."

"Oh yes, husband, I know he is," I said quickly, and then in a sudden panic, I pleaded, "But Henry, will you not feel little Henry's forehead? He feels rather warm to me."

"Hmm...." He laid a hand on Henry's head, his fingers long and pale as a starfish. "I will ask for my father's physician to wait on him, Ursula."

"Oh, yes, please, husband. We must take no chances."

"You do not need to tell me that, my dear. Wait here, and I will have Dr. Starkey attend." An anxious look had come into his eyes, and I knew that for all his faults, Henry loved little Henry just as much as I did.

He hurried from the room in pursuit of the doctor, and I breathed a heavy sigh of relief as the door closed behind him. Hugging my baby close to me, I gazed at his tiny face, seeing that it burnt as if on fire, and my heart ached until it was a physical pain. I sat then on the very edge of the nursing chair, and nervously watched the bedchamber door as I waited for the doctor to come.

~*~

I'd seen Max and Claire together many, many times now, walking along Havant High Street, Claire's step matching Max's long stride and her short skirts seeming to show even more of her slim thighs than ever before. I'd watched them shopping in Woolworths and Boots and several of the tiny groovy boutiques in the arcade, taking a leisurely walk around Havant Park, and even going into the Wetherspoons pub, The Parchment Makers, for a lunch time drink.

I'd spied on Max queuing for his lunch in Smith & Vosper, and Claire serving him, smiling broadly as she passed his coffee and sandwich over the counter. It made me wonder what else she had been serving him; I couldn't imagine that it was just coffee, sandwiches, and smiles. Rather, it probably involved something sweet and cloying, and could be either a Belgian bun or a Bavarian slice. I felt as if I was snooping around like a police officer, or like one of the private detectives that used to be on that old TV program, *Charlies Angels*. Although maybe one of Max's Devils would be a better way to describe me at the moment.

I wondered what Stuart made of all this, and whether he thought that Max and Claire were acting unprofessionally. I daren't ask him. I didn't want him to know that I had a green eyed monster sitting on my shoulder whispering mean, jealous things about the two of them in my ear, and that all I wanted was for Sarah to come back to work and for Claire to disappear back into the clutches of Smith & Vosper for good.

I constantly asked myself why I cared so much. Why did I care that Max and Claire seemed to enjoy each other's company and wanted to be together all the time? She was my sister; I should be glad that she'd found somebody to love, as Freddie Mercury used to sing when in that famous rock group Queen. The problem was, though, that when I looked at Max I saw Gregory, and wondered when I would ever see him again. (Although I must remember that wondering is for fools, as Henry Stafford had said). Centuries may go by before I got my wish to be with Gregory again, and how would I cope? The burden of my painful heart was becoming

75

far too heavy already.

It'd been a couple of weeks since the last time I visited that other world—when I'd met my husband Henry—and found it so hard to believe that he'd enticed Ursula to have fourteen children with him; one of the great mysteries of the world. I found myself becoming more and more anxious as each day went by. I worried all the time about little Henry; and what made it even worse was that, through reading all the available information on Wikipedia, I knew my baby's fate. If I had to go back as Ursula to witness that, as well as my own mother's execution, then perhaps it was for the best if I never went back at all.

A tentative enquiring voice took me away from my thoughts, and I looked up from my computer screen—which at the moment made no sense at all, the words swimming in front of me like little tadpoles—into the kind but troubled face of Stuart Rhodes.

"Are you okay, Hannah? You look as if you've the whole world balancing on those narrow shoulders of yours."

"I'm okay, Stuart. Thanks. My shoulders are a lot broader than you think." I pushed my arms akimbo like a weight lifter, and gave him an impish grin as he shrugged into his coat and, picking up his briefcase, prepared to leave the office.

He smiled as he said, "Are you feeling better now? Max said you'd not been well."

"Oh yeah, fine now, thanks."

"Good. Look, Hannah, I've gotta dash. I've got to take Izzy to Rainbows tonight, and there's a parent's meeting at the school as well."

"Have fun," I shouted after him as he dashed out of the door, his long overcoat flying behind like a cloak.

I heard a vague "See you tomorrow" and the slam of the

door as I prepared to go home. I turned off the computer, put away a few files, and tidied my desk before putting on my coat and turning off the lights, reminding myself that I must check to see that Max's office was locked before I went.

I was just walking across the tiled entrance area to the tiny front door — people back in the day must have been so much smaller — when Max's office door opened and he appeared in the doorway, making me jump out of my skin. I could almost see it, my skin, draped over the back of my chair like a coat.

For a split second I thought I'd gone back and that he was my lover, Gregory Walsh, until I saw that instead of black trousers and a tight white shirt that showed all the muscles in his chest, he looked extremely smart in a dark grey suit teamed with a thick cream shirt, a faint silver stripe running through it. He wore a tie but it was loose, and a slice of bare skin showed between the open top buttons of his shirt. I carefully averted my eyes.

"Hannah, have you got time for a quick word before you go?"

"God, Max, you made me jump," I said. "I thought you'd gone, and was just about to check your office before I locked up." I dangled a set of keys in front of him. "Is Claire with you?"

"Claire? No, of course not. She must have gone home."

"Oh," I shrugged, as I went into the office and sat down on my usual chair, putting my bag at my feet. "I've gotten so used to seeing the two of you together," I giggled inanely.

"Hmm," he replied, shutting the door and sitting down on the leather swivel chair behind his desk. "That's one of the things I want to talk to you about."

I must have looked puzzled, because he said, shaking his head slightly, "This is a bit awkward, Hannah, but the thing is, I don't know how to tell Claire that I don't want her company every lunch time—well, every minute of every day, actually." He grinned shame faced, and when I didn't say anything, said, "You must think me awful to talk about your sister like that, but—"

"No, Max, I don't, but…. You seem to enjoy being with her—I thought you two were an item."

Max shook his head, surprised. "No. No way. She's a nice girl, and a chat and a stroll around Havant Park is great sometimes. But it's every day, Hannah. She follows me around."

For some strange reason my heart rose at the thought that Max didn't fancy Claire, but all the same I said angrily, "I've seen you buying lunch in Smith & Vosper. You know she works there, so it looks to me as if you're following her too."

"No." He shook his head vehemently. "She asked me to go in, said she would get my lunch on her discount card—as a way of saying thank you for being able to talk—you know—about London and everything."

"London?" I queried.

"Oh, you don't know?" He blushed—the "I'm so great" Max Reynolds blushing again—as if the thought had suddenly occurred to him that obviously I wouldn't know.

I shook my head. "No, I know nothing about London. Well, only that she was fed up with legal work and wanted a change. What happened, Max?"

"Oh, no, no," he said, raising his hands palms up in front of him. "She told me in confidence, Hannah. No way."

"Max."

"No."

"Hmm," I said. "Well, I'll have to ask her myself then. I knew something had happened to bring her back here, and that it had to be something bad to make her leave legal work and get a job in a baker's shop. That's so unlike Claire. And her appearance has changed so much too."

"Her appearance?" he questioned.

"Yeah," I said. "I forgot, you wouldn't have seen the way she looked before she went to London."

"Actually," he pointed out, "Maybe she needs to tone it down a bit for the office. You know, the short skirts and low-cut tops."

Feeling quite riled up now for some strange reason, I replied, "She looks exactly like your usual type, Max. All the girlfriends I've ever seen you with resemble a Barbie doll."

There was a long silence; such a long silence that I thought Max would perhaps never speak to me again. He kept his blond head down, and I noticed that he fiddled nervously with the well sharpened pencils that lay in a neat row on his desk. At long last he looked up just as a shaft of bright sunlight fell through the window, illuminating his green eyes so that they glowed like emeralds.

"Yeah," he said thoughtfully. "Maybe you're right." He laughed a little and grinned wryly. "I suppose there's always been a certain look." Then he said quietly, "I admire other looks more though, Hannah."

There was another silence. I really didn't know what to say to that. Did he mean my looks? Surely not.

Before I could reply, he said softly, "I know what's been happening to you, Hannah."

Putting on a bored voice, I said, "What are you talking about, Max?"

My heart thumped painfully in my breast, and I felt as if I couldn't breathe as slowly he left his leather swivel chair and came to sit close to me, perched on the edge of the desk, his trousers stretched tight against his thighs.

Leaning forward, he clasped both my hands in his and, coming even closer, his breath feeling so warm against my neck, he whispered in my ear, "You know who I am, don't you, Hannah? I know who you are." When I didn't reply, he pulled back slightly, his hands now clasping my shoulders, and looked at my face, his gaze lingering hungrily, for what seemed like ages, on my eyes and my lips.

I gave tiny shakes of my head, feeling like one of those Churchill nodding dogs that people sit in the back of their cars. I didn't dare to speak or even breathe, my fingers splayed over my mouth. He knew who I was? He knew that I was Ursula? He knew that I went back and became Ursula Pole? Did he go back too, then? No, it couldn't be true, not Max as well as Sarah. But then he spoke again.

"Hannah, why do you think I was in the cemetery that day when you came around, the day that we kissed? Come on, Hannah, you must know — it's so obvious." And here he paused before saying, "I'm Gregory, Gregory Walsh."

I stood up so abruptly, pulling my hands from his, that my chair toppled back and lay prone like a dead body on the carpet. Anger like a red-hot light filled me from head to toe, and my heart beat so hard I felt breathless.

"Really, Max? Is that the best you can do?" I said scathingly. "Are you jumping on the band wagon? What are you going fob me off with next? That Stuart goes back as Henry Stafford, Ursula's mincing husband?"

"Please, Hannah, listen…."

Max put out his hands but I ignored them and, turning, fled across the room, looking back only once to see him wincing, fingers splayed across his eyes. Wrenching at the door, I stalked through, letting it close with an almighty crash.

Chapter Eight

I gazed out of the massive bay window of my bedchamber at Warblington Manor, watching the snow as it fell thick and fast, concealing the lawns and the lush flower beds beneath its thick white cover. Flakes twirled through the air like tiny dancing fairies, and rimmed the skeletal branches of the trees as if with a deep layer of fur, reminding me of the sable edged cloak that I had wrapped around my grieving body at my baby Henry's funeral that very day. My heart lay heavy as a stone in my breast as I thought of him lying so pale and still in the dark dismal crypt in St. Thomas à Becket Church. I wrung my hands with misery.

We had travelled for days, the long journey from London to Warblington, in the jolting coach, with Henry's tiny body in its casket, the poor horses' hooves stumbling over stones and their skinny legs knee deep in slimy, stinking mud, for the snow had not yet begun then. I thanked God that my mother resided in Warblington Manor, for when the temperature dropped and the snow began to fall, the way back to London became totally impossible, and we were so glad to have a roof over our heads and food in our bellies.

Depending on how long the snow stayed, it could be

many months before we were able to return to London, and the thought that I would be close to my mother for that length of time sustained me for now, although I knew that Henry would want to return as soon as possible. I was aware that I should make the most of this time, but my grief was disabling me, and taking pleasure from everything that I normally loved.

The snow was a blizzard now, and I had a sudden panicked thought that my baby Henry would be cold in his lead lined coffin, and that I should have put a warm scarf around his neck and cozy booties on his bare feet. I wished that he was there now, lying in my arms and blowing bubbles from between his rosebud lips, his blossoming smile a cheeky ray of sunshine. I had an urge to run out into the snow and creep through the eerie graveyard amongst leaning tombstones, and from there to the crypt where my baby lay sleeping forever and ever. My heart pounded with terror.

I curbed this desire, for Henry, my husband, watched my every move, and any irrational behavior from me would be cause for him to speak to his father, Lord Buckingham, and then perhaps the king, and I had a dread of them conspiring together and locking me away. My mother was always there for me, but in this world of powerful men, there was only so much that she could do.

The door swung open and Henry minced into the room, his whole attire, particularly his long skinny legs in black hose, an affront to my attraction to Gregory Walsh. "Ah, Ursula you are here. Have you nothing to do, wife, but stare from the window at the falling snow? Rouse yourself. You are neglecting your needle skills and your music, my dear. You know how much you love your music."

Leaden hearted, I gazed at him, wondering if he, as much

as I, missed our son, Henry. Our beautiful boy, who used to lay in his crib waving chubby arms and legs, and awakening the whole household by bawling his head off before the sun, in a crimson glow, had risen from behind banked clouds.

Somehow guessing my thoughts, Henry came closer and, unusual for him, put a comforting hand on my shoulder. "We cannot replace our boy, wife, but there will be more children in time."

The thought of the years to come spent in bearing Henry's children filled me with the utmost dismay; and how must it be for him too? After all, his pleasure lay in the bodies of men, not women, and it must be as much of a trial for him to bed me as I to bed him. For Henry, though, as most men, heirs were of the greatest importance compared to any feelings they may have for a mere wife.

I nodded and tried to raise a smile, and Henry, encouraged, said, "Your harp strings will stiffen, wife, if you do not pluck them. Now you are here in your childhood home and have access to your instruments, you should practice."

I nodded and said, "Yes, husband, I will go to the music room and practice for a while." I bobbed him a curtsey and began to leave the room, Henry informing me as I went that he would be with my father and brothers in the great hall. They were to meet before dinner was served.

My beautiful harp stood still and solitary on the stone flags of the music room. The room was chilly, and no fire burned in the grate. As I hadn't been there and my brothers had limited musical ability, it would have been a long time since anybody entered this room.

A snow shower splattered heavily against the window as I sat on the stool and positioned the harp between my legs. Running my fingers gently over the strings, I picked out one of my favorite tunes, *Greensleeves*, which instead of bringing me the comfort I had hoped for, grieved me more. The pain in my breast over the loss of my baby intensified, as well as the longing to see Gregory. I knew that he lived in a cottage with his father and sister on the grounds of Warblington Manor. Surely it would not be too hard to find.

Overcome by the desire for the irrational behavior that I knew I should avoid, I sprung to my feet and rushed from the room, my feet flying down the stairs and into the hallway, where I grabbed a cloak, wrapped it around my body, and pulled the hood up over my head. I crept stealthily to the back of the house, through the main kitchen and scullery, which was quiet at this time of day, and from there out of the back door and into the garden, hoping against hope that nobody had seen me. I would certainly pay a high price if Henry found out where I was going.

A blast of icy air hit me immediately and I sunk to my knees into deep snow, my thin slippers and the hem of my black mourning gown becoming soaked through. As if wading through deep sludgy water, I made my way over to a nearby copse of trees, silhouetted bright white against a glacial sky. They looked familiar, and I thought from there I could follow the path through the woods. Hopefully it was the right path, as everything looked alien to me, the snow having turned the landscape into a blurry haze.

I trudged on through the deep snow for what seemed like hours, when all of a sudden I saw a plume of smoke spiraling up into the air and a snow covered cottage came into view, its windows peeking out like glassy eyes from beneath the overhanging snow laden thatch. Almost collapsing with exhaustion and relief, I banged on the sturdy wooden door. It opened swiftly and there he was, Gregory, my love Gregory, the surprise evident in his eyes as he stared at me.

"Ursula." Grabbing hold of my arm, he pulled me into the warmth of the cottage and slammed the door shut. "Good God, woman, where have you come from? Are you an apparition?"

Stammering and crying, my teeth chattering with the cold, I tried to explain as Gregory helped me with my cloak, pushed the hood back from my face, and smiled with relief when he saw that it is unmarked from my husband's cruel hands. He took my own freezing hands between his and pulled me into his warm embrace. A bright red fire crackled and burned in the fireplace as he helped me to a chair and settled me there, while pushing a cup of hot broth to my lips. Melted snow dripped onto the floor, soaking the sweet scented rushes.

"I had to come, Gregory," I told him between sobs. "Oh God, I need you. My baby Henry has died, and my grief is unbearable."

"Oh Ursula, Ursula." He rocked me gently, his lips raining kisses on my damp hair. "It was the smallpox then?"

I nodded yes, and then a voice intervened.

"Ah, so this is the fair Ursula then, son?"

"Ursula, this is my father, Isaac." I took him in, feasting on him, seeing the resemblance and the source of Gregory's good looks. "And my sister, Alice." I couldn't see her at first, but peering from behind Isaac there was a girl, her hair long, well past her shoulders, and glinting fair in the snowy light from the window. Her skin looked as smooth as porcelain, and she had a deep dimple in her chin below lips as plump as pillows.

I tried to stand up to honor them with a curtsy, but Gregory held me back, saying, "No, Ursula, take care. You are too weak."

85

Gregory was right. My legs quivered unsteadily as I tried to stand, so I sunk back down into the cushions and said, "It's so good to meet you both at last." They walked towards me, but Alice reached me first, and as her hand touched my arm she began to fade very slowly, her vibrant colors becoming muted. The room spun, and I was as giddy as if on a twirling carousel, painted horses bobbing up and down, up and down.

"Hey, Hannah?"

A hand waved in front of my vision, but I ignore it and turned back to where I thought Gregory was. I longed to nestle into the warmth of his body. I was still cold from my snowy walk, my hands and feet freezing, my fingers and toes still numb. To my surprise, though, sunlight poured through the window, and I saw that the snow had stopped falling and the air was warm. I flexed my fingers and toes and reveled in the heat, and looked up at a sky that was bright with skeins of creamy clouds dotted all over the blue.

A face floated above me, and with some disappointment I saw that it wasn't Gregory — not my dear Gregory — nor even Max, but Sarah. She looked worried, a deep vee creased into the space between her eyebrows. I looked around and saw that we were in the sitting room at Mitchell Road, and that the clock on the mantelpiece was ticking very loudly, its golden pendulum swinging backwards and forwards, backwards and forwards.

"Sarah — oh, Sarah," I said to her. "My baby has died, my baby Henry."

"Hey, Hannah, I know it seems very real to you, but it's Ursula's baby. Ursula's baby has died."

"But I am Ursula," I told her violently. "I am Ursula Pole." I burst into noisy sobs, tears running in sluggish trails down my burning cheeks. "Help me, Sarah, you must help me, for I feel so alone." I held out my hands.

~*~

Claire had texted me and asked if I'd like to meet for a drink—she needed to talk to me, she said. *Hmm*, I thought to myself. *Is she going to tell me the whole sorry tale about what happened in London?* Hopefully she would, otherwise curiosity was going to get the better of me and I'd have to sit Max in a cold miserable room on a hard, wooden chair beneath a naked burning light bulb, and torture him to get the full story.

Max, I thought. *Max Reynolds, who has spun me a pretty tale about him going back in time as well and being, of all people, Gregory Walsh.* There was no way in this world—or the other world, come to that—that I believed a word of it. He must have thought I was born yesterday—or indeed in the 1500s. Haha, how funny am I? He must have heard me say something about a Gregory. Actually, yes, I remembered him asking me once if I had a boyfriend called Gregory, so yes, he had heard the name. I must have said something when I was coming around in the office the very first time I had a time travel experience.

He was obviously having a bit of fun with me, a bit of a tease. Typical of Max. But hey—as Sarah would say—I was not going to let him get the better of me that was for sure. Just one thing was bothering me, though. How did he know the name Gregory Walsh? Yeah, okay, he could have gotten the name Gregory from my ramblings, but I didn't think I'd said his surname. In fact, I knew that I hadn't. So how did he know?

Anyway, back to Claire, I really wanted to find out what had brought her back to Havant. As far as I was aware—and Mum and Dad too, I thought—she had loved London and never wanted to leave. I'd always thought that London suited

Claire so well, and that was before her transformation into Barbie, so something really serious must have happened to change her mind.

As I got ready to meet my sister, I mulled over the last time I'd gone back and the trauma of losing baby Henry. It had taken me a long time to get over the experience, and I found myself waking in the early hours, my heart galloping as hard as the horses that had pulled our coach on that awful long journey from London to St. Thomas à Becket Church, with Henry in his tiny white coffin.

I kept picturing his little face, so pinched and pale, sunken within the folds of the sumptuous pale blue satin that lined his casket. I was trying to take Sarah's advice, and reminded myself that it was Ursula's baby that had died and not mine, but, oh God, how hard it was to make myself believe that.

The trauma of the birth also kept running through my mind, and, indeed, the fact that I — or Ursula, I should say — had almost died. All that pain and suffering, and for what? A poor dead baby that would eventually crumble to nothing but dust and decay? Hunching my shoulders against a sudden shiver along my spine, and trying to clear my mind of all things connected to the 1500s, I checked that I had everything I needed, all the essentials — my bag, my phone, a bottle of water, my keys — and went to my car to drive to Havant.

The Wetherspoons pub The Parchment Makers was busy, but I spied Claire straight away, sitting at a table for two by the window, intently studying the menu. She was wearing her usual Barbie uniform of a very short skirt and low-necked top, teamed with a short leather biker jacket decorated with silver studs and a massive fur collar. She looked as if she had a black fluffy cat curled around her neck.

Looking up and seeing me, she raised her hand in greeting

and said, "Hannah, do you want to look at the menu before going to the bar? I'm starving, and some of the food comes with a free drink."

"Hi, Claire. Yes, okay; I'm a bit hungry too."

I sat down opposite her. We chatted about this and that as we decided what to order, and then Claire said that she would treat me—which came as something of a shock—so she went off to the bar, taking the massive plastic menu with her. The pub was a hubbub of noise, with diners at nearly every table, most with a high chair beside them and children running around as if in a kindergarten. Some of the tables hadn't been cleared and were littered with a jumble of dirty plates and smeary glasses.

I noticed a couple of men and women at a nearby table eyeballing Claire as she walked back to our table, her belt masquerading as a skirt, wriggling further and further up her thighs as if it had come alive. A skinny waitress, clad all in black, a look of panic in her eyes, raced past with plates of burgers and chips laid along both arms, almost tripping over a baby crawling on the floor like a clockwork doll.

"It's a bit manic in here, isn't?" I said to Claire as she put two glasses of red wine on the table.

She sat down opposite me and said, "Yeah, maybe we should have gone to our local The Old House at Home, or perhaps The Bear. But it's so cheap in here."

I took a sip of wine before saying, "Well, I just hope the food is good."

"Yeah, it is. The veggie burger is lovely. I've had it a couple of times with Max."

"Oh yes," I said sarcastically. "The Max that you don't like because he's up himself?"

She laughed and said, "Yeah. Well, things aren't always

as they seem, are they, Hannah?"

"What do you mean by that? And what about you, Claire Palmer? You, who have spent the past few weeks shamelessly flirting with him. Actually, it makes me wonder if you two aren't an item."

"Well, what I mean by that is—Max and I think that you've been acting strange lately. Maybe having some sort of other worldly experiences. And I also think you're jealous of me flirting with Max. You like him, Hannah—it stands out a mile."

I felt a tiny hurt stab at the thought of Max talking about me to Claire, but said calmly enough, "Of course I like him, as a boss. But that's it." And then with a bit more venom, I added, "Take no notice of what Max says. Things are not as they seem with him either. Actually, he complained to me about the amount of time that he's had to spend with you—says that you follow him around."

She glanced up quickly, "He never said that."

Before I could reply the panicky looking waitress arrived with the food and, dumping it down on the table in front of us, said, really really quickly, "Hopeyouenjoyyourfood"—or something like that—before rushing away and once again almost tripping over the clockwork baby, who was making her way ungainly over a floor littered with discarded greasy chips and hunks of rapidly hardening bread.

Using her fork to poke around at the burger and chips in front of her, Claire said, "Well, whatever, it won't matter soon because I'm going to be leaving." She speared a chip, put it in her mouth, and began chewing rapidly.

I bit into my burger which, as Claire had said, tasted really good, and said, "Leaving? You mean because Sarah's coming back to work next week?"

"Well, yeah. But I'm leaving Smith & Vosper too." She took a deep glug of wine.

I stopped mid chew and gazed at her. "Why?"

"Well.... look, Hannah, I'm going to tell you everything now." She laid her knife and fork on her barely touched plate and, sitting back in her chair, took a deep breath. Her phone, which was on the table beside her, suddenly beeped and a text message popped up. She glanced at it quickly and smiled.

Well, well, I thought. *At last I'm going to find out what had happened in London.* "Have you already told Max about this?" I asked her, and then, noticing her almost full plate, said, "I thought you said you were hungry?"

She nodded and assured me that she had told Max, and then began to poke at her front teeth with her finger as if she had food stuck there. When she'd finished with that, she speared another chip and chewed again. "I am, but I need to tell you this before I can concentrate on the food. I'm a bit nervous."

"Nervous? Why? Is it bad news?" I held up my glass of wine. "Do I need to drink some more of this to fortify me?"

She laughed, and was just about to speak when the panicky waitress appeared again and said, "Isyourfoodokay?" or something like that, before rushing off before we could either shake or nod our heads.

We leaned in towards each other, and Claire, glancing nervously over her shoulder, said softly, "Hannah, I left London and legal work and came back to Havant because I was having an affair with somebody—my boss, actually—and their partner found out."

I couldn't help it—my mouth gaped open like a trap door, and I said, "Good God, Claire. Go on."

"Well, the thing is, I've been in touch with this person

all the time I've been here. We've missed each other and....
well, they've decided to leave their partner for me so that we
can make a go of it together." She picked up a chip with her
fingers and began to nibble at it delicately, and then swallowed
another healthy slug of wine.

"That's good news in a way—for you," I stammered.
"You said partner. Are they married?"

Claire nodded. "Yes, of course it's good news, and yes,
they're married. I know that it must all sound a bit messy
to you, but we love each other, Hannah." She gazed at me
imploringly.

My food forgotten for the time being, I took another sip
of wine and asked, "Aren't you going to tell me who he is?
What's his name?"

The noise in the pub seemed to intensify, and the small
child sitting at the next table began to scream and bang her
heels against the rungs of her chair. I leaned forward even
closer so that I could hear Claire's very low voice, and for the
first time in ages noticed that Claire's eyes weren't blue like
Max's Barbie dolls, but hazel, just like mine.

She focused on her plate, staring at it really hard for
what seemed ages, before looking at me intently and saying,
"Hannah, I don't know what you're going to think, but the
thing is.... It's not a he, but a she, and her name's Laura." I
think I must have simply stared at her, my eyes wide, because
she said, "So, Hannah, you can rest assured that Max and I
are definitely not an item."

Chapter Nine

A split second ago I was Hannah Palmer, busily working in the garden at Mitchell Road, weeding the borders and cutting back the roses, trying to be extra careful with the thorny branches that pulled at my skin, drawing blood that bloomed into little scarlet beads on my fingers. The sun glowing from a deep blue sky felt warm on my back, and the smell of the roses — bright yellows, reds, and pinks — suffused the air with their sweet scent.

Tiny, dainty steps had taken me from one world into the other, and I was now Ursula Pole again. I was somewhere dark and dank within thick walls, with the smell of muddy water creeping through the stone like a poisonous gas. My mother, Margaret Pole, kneeled at a makeshift altar on the cold hard stone, her back ramrod straight and her gnarled hands steepled together, muttering under her breath, a long low monotonous sound. I thought she was praying — praying for her life. She was much older now, her face seamed and the tiny stray hairs peeking from her hood as grey as old iron, yet she still retained a presence, an aura, an almost ghostly aura. It shone around her in this gloomy place like a silver halo.

She stood up, keeping a hand on her lower back as if

she was in pain and, bobbing her head, walked slowly and carefully through an arch in the thick walls and into the adjoining cell. In keeping with her noble birth, the cell had been made as comfortable as it could be for a person being held within the confines of the dreaded Tower of London, for this was surely where I was now.

I saw that the thick walls were adorned with hangings, and the floor in sweet scented rushes. My mother's bed was a lush four poster affair covered with a thick counterpane, and there was a chair and a writing table laden with books next to a tiled washstand. A porcelain chamber pot glinted beneath the bed. A heavy tome of a Bible lay on the chair, and candles streaked with knobs of wax glimmered in the dim.

My mother had but one gown and hardly any underclothes to speak of, and these were tired and worn now. But oh, how thoughtful King Henry had been in the two and half years that he had kept an innocent woman here against her will. I didn't know how she had been able to withstand this confinement, for even standing on tiptoes, I could only just see a sliver of blue sky from the tiny slit of a window, and feel only a stirring of warm air against my face.

I suspected that it was spring time, yet here there was no smell of new growth and no sunshine pouring in from the outside. The odor of death, decay, and despair seeped from the very walls, and I realized with an awful sinking heart that today, because there was no escape, I would have to witness my mother, Margaret Pole's, execution. Oh my God, how would this be borne?

My mother, my poor poor mother, confined for so long in such a deep dark place. Mother...a lover of laughter and song, who enjoyed the warmth of the sun on her skin and the sound of raindrops pattering through leafy trees. Who loved to see the sun rising and setting in a crimson hue, and rainbows arching across a rain-washed sky. My mother, who kept my secrets and let me grow, always, within her heart.

My heart thumped now like a drum as I heard the tramping of feet on the stairs, and immediately melted deep within the shadows of the cell. The heavy metal door creaked open and a slovenly maid walked in, a silver plate in her hand, which she clattered onto the small table. I saw that it was some sort of thin gruel swimming with grease, skinny white meat floating on its surface. She gave a short, perfunctory bow of the head and then backed out, locking the door behind her with a magnificent silver key.

My mother sat on the chair, her dark threadbare gown belling around her legs, holding on tightly to the Bible. She stared at the food then looked away, sickened, it seemed, by its oily stench. She could not see me—I was invisible. I was an imposter, a visitor from another time, another world, just as I had been when I witnessed the soldiers forcibly dragging her from Warblington Manor to bring her here to wait these many years for her death day. It seemed there was nothing I could do to help her. She would be alone today.

It was later, much later, for the sun had moved and was a distant yellow glow at the tiny window. Once again there were footsteps on the steep stairs, and the cell door swung open, admitting the constable of the tower. I watched, from the shadows, this short burly man, who had narrow, flinty blue eyes and a beard that coated his chin like well clipped hedging.

He informed my mother in a booming voice, "Margaret Pole, Countess of Salisbury, I am here to inform you that your death by beheading will take place this day, the twenty-seventh of May in the year of our Lord, fifteen forty-one. Your crime is treason against Henry the Eighth, King of England. I will return for you within the hour."

"No crime can be proven against me," my mother replied, springing up from the chair in shock, it seemed, as I saw feelings of anger and despair in equal measure passing rapidly across her face.

Giving a slight bow of his head, he went from the room with not another word, clanging the door shut behind him. She paced then, backwards and forwards, backwards and forwards across the stone flagged floor, her soft slippers whispering amongst the rushes. And then she lay upon her bed, the Bible clutched in both hands and her eyes closed. I could see the panicked rise and fall of her breasts against the worn silk of her gown.

The awful long hour passed, and then, as promised, the silver key grated in the lock and the door creaked open. Then pandemonium ensued as they surged in, filling the dank cell with their noxious stench. I flattened myself into the shadows, the stone wall behind me deathly cold, watching as the huddle of stinking, smelling men grabbed her from her bed and rushed her from the room, almost dragging my poor old mother, pious Margaret Pole, down the steep stone steps.

Hurrying after them, I sped down the stairs, my heart hammering in my throat and my hands shaking in despair. *How can I stop this?* I thought to myself. *How can I stop this terrible act of atrocity?*

Outside the sun blazed from a porcelain blue sky, and leafy trees waved their branches in a gentle spring breeze. The men, huffing and puffing from exertion, dragged my mother, her face a mask of despair, not to a scaffold as I had thought, but to a simple wooden block which had been placed on the soft spring grass. Guards and the executioner, a young man clutching an axe in his quivering hands, surrounded her. Nervous sweat coated the executioner's upper lip.

The small crowd made up of officials and workers from the tower were tense with anticipation, whispering amongst themselves, and I made to step forward, to speak for her, when a voice said in my ear—or was it just in my head? — "You can't change history, Ursula. Do not tempt fate."

I heard her voice then, pleading, desperate, old and reedy, yet cutting swiftly through the muttering of the crowd. "Where is the king? I must speak with the king, with Henry. He is my kin." She scanned the crowd with eyes as frightened as a cornered animal, and when nobody replied, she said staunchly, "No crime can be proven against me."

Then she became silent, as did the crowd, and I watched as she proudly stood tall, her palms pressed together at her chest and her mouth moving in prayer. There was a deep dark silence where nobody moved and nothing stirred. If a pin had dropped the sound would have been as cannon fire. And then, even as I blinked, my mother was pushed to a kneeling position and her head, her poor thin neck exposed to the sweet smelling air, lay in readiness on the block as the axe arced through the air, glinting in the sunshine.

And then I came around and was sitting in my garden in a flower bed, squashed in amongst the pom pom dahlias and the roses, thorny branches clutched tightly in my scratched hands. I watched in shock as my blood seeped into the earth, just as my mother's, Margaret Pole's, had when it gushed in a crimson hue from her neck such a long, long time ago. I felt heavy with despair until I looked up and saw that Gregory was there—or was it Max? —and he held out his arms and, whimpering, I fell into them.

~*~

For traitors on the block should die. I am no traitor no, not I....

These words ran through my head as I parked my car along the road by the row of cottages at Langstone just before the Ship Inn. I was planning on a walk along the shoreline past the Old Mill and the Royal Oak public house, and so on to Warblington Cemetery and St. Thomas à Becket Church. I had an urge to visit the ruin again, to place my hands on the cold slumbering stones, and like a magician, conjure up Margaret Pole and bring her back to life.

I needed to go back to a time before she died, before cruel King Henry stole her life away from her, and to a time when she was vibrant and alive and she was my mother.

My faithfulness stands and so, towards the block I shall not go.

The last couple of lines of the poem come to mind as I set off, my rucksack bouncing jauntily on my back, making sure that I set my Fitbit to the walk mode. I was determined to start trying to get my steps in every day.

Nor make one step, as you shall see, Christ in Thy mercy, save Thou me.

According to Wikipedia, this poem had been found scratched into the stone in Margaret Pole's cell in the Tower of London. She had made it clear right up to the end that she was innocent of any wrongdoing. Surely Henry should have known that, and should have trusted her as a close member of his family. After all, he had allowed her to be godmother to Queen Mary, and she had cared for both Mary and Elizabeth as a nanny for many years. Poor, misunderstood lady.

Flashbacks of the execution kept coming into my mind, and the sight of the poor bowed figure of Margaret Pole, her head on the block and the axe hitting not her neck as it was supposed to, but her shoulders and her back, tormented me. She had tried to escape, had crawled away, her wounds leaving a bloody trail on the grass. The young man, the executioner, the heavy axe shaking within his grasp, had followed behind, hacking at her violently like the Grim Reaper.

I stood and gazed at the lovely view, desperately trying to rid myself of such macabre thoughts, and finding it hard to believe that the execution of Margaret Pole had actually taken place. Thoughts of Gregory and Max came to me, and how sure I'd been that one of them, particularly Max, had been there when I'd come round after witnessing the execution. How sure I'd been that I was in Max's arms, when really there was nobody there, nobody at all. It was all in my imagination. Luckily Sarah was at home, and had rushed outside to comfort me when I'd fallen to the ground, bruising my hands and my knees and sobbing uncontrollably.

Looking up, I saw that the sky was a perfect blue, only faint skeins of clouds marring its surface. The sun, which was warm for the end of May, shone in a lemon hue, and I was really glad I'd worn just shorts and a T-shirt, even though my sad winter white skin was now exposed to the air for everybody to see. My boots felt good, comfy as slippers, as I walked along the beach, searching for tiny iridescent shells that sparkled in the sun, and trying not to slip and slide on patches of slimy seaweed.

People chattering in groups sat on the stony shore eating sandwiches or enjoying a liquid lunch of beer or wine. Glamorous swans, like models on a catwalk, swayed over the stones, begging for sandwiches, nuts, and crisps, and gaggles of geese gave the quacking ducks sly nasty hisses as they paddled at the water's edge. The sea was calm and clear, and tiny waves of frothy white frill rolled to the shore. I breathed in the fresh briny odor and carried on walking along the shore, and then across fields of patchwork black and white cows and fluffy sheep until I reached the cemetery.

The graveyard was peaceful, as it always was, its tranquility marred by my hurrying footsteps as I walked past its endless rows of monuments and headstones. I loitered at the nun's plot with its simple wooden crosses. Sister Angelique, Sister Monica Jones, Sister Marguerite, Sister Bernadette — oh, how the relics of the dead went on and on. I walked past St. Thomas à Becket Church, squatting amidst its ancient graveyard, lingering only for a moment at the heart shaped headstone of Gregory's mother, Eliza Walsh, the memorial that I was so proud to have found

Claire's news came fleetingly into my mind, and I shook my head at my own stupidity in thinking that Max and Claire were together, when all the time Claire's married lover was a woman. How come I hadn't known that my own sister was gay? The whole Barbie look had been a total red herring.

"Why didn't you tell me?" I remembered asking her after she'd dropped her bombshell. "Don't you trust me, Claire?"

Gazing at me hard and putting her hand in mine, she said, "Of course I trust you, Hannah. You're my sister. But this was just too much — too much of a secret to even speak of — and I had no idea what you'd think."

"I think," I told her carefully, "That whatever makes you happy makes me happy too. When can we all meet Laura?"

Glancing at my Fitbit, I saw that I'd walked 9,522 steps. Wow. Only a few more to go now, though, because the ruin was visible, and even from this distance I could see with excitement that the gate was open so access was still possible. I would be able once again to touch the stones of what was once, such a long time ago, Warblington Manor.

With a sense of anticipation, I walked towards it and, squinting, raising my hand to block out the bright sun that shone in my eyes, I saw a figure leaning casually against the tower. As I got closer I realized that it was a man—a good looking man, wearing jeans and a white T-shirt that fit very snugly over his broad chest. His blond hair gleamed like gold, and his face was creased in a smile.

He raised his hand in a wave, and as he prowled towards me like a sleek panther, said, "Hannah. I thought you'd never come—I've been waiting for you."

Chapter Ten

Heavy with despair, my heart a cold stone in my breast, I paced the beautiful gardens at Warblington Manor. I followed the paved path around the tidy lawn and the flower beds rioting with color. There was a nippy autumn chill in the air even though it was only September, and I huddled into my warm cloak like a mouse into hibernation as I walked further and further into the outlying woods, deeper and deeper into the gloomy shade of leafy trees, away from the house — away from the blank shut windows and prying eyes that I suspected were there, but that I could not see.

King Henry had found me a husband. I knew not who he was or from where he came, but I knew that he was intended for me. All the while my heart yearned for Gregory, and I could not be true to another. It was my father who had spoken of this, who'd told my mother while I stood upstairs on our vast rectangular landing, my ear pressed to the great wooden door of his bedchamber. I wished I had heeded my mother's advice, for she had always told me that good news never came from eavesdropping.

I was here now searching for Gregory. I needed to see him, to touch him, be reassured by him that, even though there must be another, that he would not forsake me. My gown swept the leaves that were already slowly falling from the trees and lay in crispy heaps upon the ground. The air smelled smoky and woody, as dense as logs and coals burning brightly in a grate. In the orchard apples and pears hung heavy and ripe from bowed branches, and their odor, rich as a jug of cider, followed me as I walked.

I could not see Gregory anywhere—he was in none of his usual places. He was not digging the borders, the muscles in his arms rippling as he worked, or on his knees weeding, nor cutting back the roses or scything the lawns. He was not even in the little stone shed where the gardening implements were kept. I dared not go to the little cottage where he lived with his father and his sister. I felt that to go there would not be right. To go there would be a last resort.

I carried on walking, hurrying along, my soft little slippers kicking through dirt and leaves and becoming scuffed at the toes, when I heard a panicked voice behind me. "Ursula, sweetheart, wait for me."

My mother, Margaret Pole, rushed after me, her dark cloak flowing behind like wings, the hood pulled up over her hair, tiny curls of which had escaped from the confines of her net and glistened wetly in the sunlight. She was out of breath, and placed a hand on my arm as we both stopped under the shade of overhanging trees.

She was much younger, her face clear and unlined, and her eyes shone very blue. "I need to speak with you," she said. "Come, let us sit in the walled garden. We can enjoy the last of the sunshine there."

Dust motes, like tiny fairies, danced in the patch of sunlight surrounding the stone bench as my mother and I sat in the walled garden, our beautiful gowns belling around us like flowers. Birds chirped and squawked in the drowsy air, and I found myself perspiring under my arms and in the crease between my breasts. The walled garden was indeed a sun trap.

"I will waste no time, but cut to the quick," she whispered to me. "King Henry has found you a husband."

I bowed my head, hoping to hide my face from my all-seeing mother, but she guessed straight away and, giggling like a girl, chided me, saying, "Ursula—you already know. Have you been eavesdropping again? Listening at doors will do you no good, you know."

"I know, my mother, for the news can only be bad. Who is he?"

"He is Henry Stafford, 1st Baron Stafford, son of the 3rd Duke of Buckingham. I think he will make a good match, my Ursula, so you need not fear."

I had heard of him, heard of his name, but asked, "Is he much older than me, Mother?"

She shook her head. "No, only perhaps three summers older."

"Does my father approve?"

"Yes, my Little Bear. Your father approves."

I must have looked sad and pensive for, glancing around first of all, she whispered, so close that her breath tickled my ear, making me hunch my shoulders to my ears, "I know that you love another, but believe me Ursula that love can never be a true match. He is a fine, good-looking man, but he is too low born for you, not of your station. It would never be allowed, not only by the king, but your father too."

I knew all this already, and was aware that Gregory and I were a dream too good to be true, but for the harsh reality to be put so bluntly and so finally made my heart beat with terror.

"I saw you with him," she carried on whispering. "The day the king came unannounced. Do you remember?"

I nodded, recalling that day in my mind. The day that the sun had glowed so hot and heavy in a clear blue sky. The day that my heart had felt light and free, and Gregory and I, embracing beneath the shade of leafy green trees, had heard the sound of the king's fanfare as the royal coach, lurching across the drawbridge, had rattled onto the grounds of Warblington Manor. I'd thought that we hadn't been seen, but we had.

"I will keep your secret, Ursula, my daughter, my love," my mother told me, squeezing my hand hard, so hard it almost hurt. "Yes, your secret is safe with me till the day I die."

My mother's words echoed around and around in my head as I came back to my time, my small corner of the world, and found myself at work at Reynolds & Rhodes. Oh my God, I was in Max's office — how weird — sitting on the floor surrounded by papers. Had I been in the middle of filing? I couldn't remember a thing, and apart from a slightly queasy feeling in my stomach I felt fine. At least the room wasn't spinning as it usually did, and thanked God that Max wasn't there at the moment. I picked myself up from the floor and, leaving the papers just as they were, fled from the room and went straight to the ladies' room.

Gazing into the mirror, I was amazed that I looked exactly the same as usual. My dark shoulder length hair was styled as it always was, my fringe cut straight above my eyebrows, and my face, apart from a few freckles across the nose, unblemished and serene. I heard my mother's words again. "I will keep your secret till the day I die." Little did she know how her death, so cruel and heartless, would haunt me in all the centuries to come.

Leaving the ladies' room I went back to my desk. Normal office noise surrounded me; telephones ringing, faint voices from upstairs, and keys clacking from Sarah's office next door. Had Sarah come back to work, or was Claire still here? I couldn't remember if Claire had actually left or not.

I heard the front door screech open and heavy footsteps sound across the tiled entrance way. Was that Max coming in at last? Checking my Fitbit, I saw that it was barely nine o'clock in the morning, yet he usually arrived at work a lot earlier than that. Trying not to but looking anyway, I saw that my Fitbit showed a very discouraging number of steps. I really must try to improve.

A sudden vague memory came to me of taking a walk around Langstone Shore so that I could visit the ruin again. Had Max been there? Had we gone back together? Sitting down heavily on my chair I put my fingers to my temples, but they were shaking so badly I had to drop my head into my hands. All the events, past and present, seemed to be merging into one, and my memory was becoming so poor.

I kept awaking to the sound of a baby crying, and sometimes I felt cramps and sharp needle like pains in my stomach and my lower back as I had when giving birth to baby Henry. My mother, Margaret Pole, was constantly whispering in my ear her news at the moment that King Henry had found me a husband, and in my dreams the axe fell again and again onto her poor, unresisting neck.

If that had been Max coming in to work, I really must go and see him. It was time that we had a talk. Purposefully I went from the office and through the entrance way, and then, giving a couple of sharp raps with my knuckles on Max's door and without waiting for an answering voice, I went in.

~*~

As I eased open the door the first thing I noticed was that the massive Salvador Dali painting wasn't on the wall, and the large oval mirror which usually hung over the fireplace was now a smaller square one, in which I could see the reflection of a woman with an intricate updo and wearing a long gown, over which hung a heavy cloak. This woman looked vaguely familiar, and as I walked closer and closer still, I saw with a strange sense of recognition that even though it was me, Hannah Palmer, I was Ursula Pole again.

It was a bright day yet a fire burned in the grate, the orange and red tongues of flame jostling madly up the chimney. A slumbering black cat was curled tight as a ball on the hearth. I had said that I would never come here, to this cottage, to Gregory's cottage. That it would be wrong and that it would be the last resort, but I had no choice. Fate had brought me here.

I felt as though I was split in two, and was part Hannah and part Ursula, for I knew that I had been here before on a snowy day just after my baby Henry had died, when I had met Isaac and Alice, Gregory's father and sister. But I also knew that Ursula knew none of this yet. She knew nothing of Baby Henry. I had come into an earlier time in Ursula's life, and all she knew now was that her heart was sore and she was afraid because King Henry had found her a husband, and she needed to tell Gregory her woeful tale.

There was no sign of Isaac or Alice as quietly I shut the door. The cat stood up, stretched lazily, and stared at me with bright green eyes before licking its glossy fur with a tiny pink tongue.

"Gregory?" I called, "Gregory, are you here?"

I heard brisk movement overhead and then footsteps

clattering on the steep stone stairs, and Gregory appeared in the doorway, a huge smile on his handsome face. He wore his usual attire of black trousers and tight white shirt, and he must have been in the middle of washing, for as I pressed myself against him his skin smelt pleasantly damp and soapy.

"Ursula? What brings you here?" He pulled me down on the settee, taking hold of my small hands in his large ones.

"Are you alone?" I asked him.

He nodded. "Yes, for a while. My father and sister are at market for the day, and I am here because my work in the garden is finished for now. What is it, Ursula, Little Bear? Has bad news brought you here?"

"Yes. My mother has told me that the king has found me a husband." Not being able to sit still for want of going mad, I stood up abruptly and began pacing up and down. The black cat watched me, its tiny head moving from side to side.

He jumped up too and took hold of me, putting his hands on my shoulders, forcing me to face him. "This was bound to happen at some point," he said. "You are of age. Who is he?"

"Henry Stafford," I told him, and then, almost sobbing, said, "I know not who he is or even what he looks like. How can I bear to kiss a man who isn't you."

Pulling me closer still, Gregory said with a frown, "Henry Stafford? I have seen him — a mincer of a man. Does he not favor men?"

"What do you mean?" I asked him, an innocent at but fifteen years old.

"A man who is a man but not a man," Gregory replied. And when I looked at him so openly, so young and so trusting, all he could say was, "The world is a cruel place, Ursula."

The two of us being alone together and entwined so closely was tantalizing, and as his gaze lingered on my mouth and mine on his, our passions rose and we kissed, our tongues entwining, dancing in each other's mouths.

"Come to bed with me, Ursula, my love," he crooned in my ear, and willingly, our hands clasped tightly together, I followed him up the steep stone steps and into his bedchamber, which was set in the thatched roof amongst the eaves. Nesting birds twittered and fluttered as, very slowly, he removed my gown and my underclothes until I was naked beneath him and he naked above me. The heat of his skin scorched mine like the warmth of the fire that burned in the grate downstairs.

Erotically he licked my neck and nibbled my earlobes, his tongue moving to my lips, where he pushed it hard and deep into my mouth until I moaned with delight. Gazing into each other's eyes, I climbed on top of him, my breasts brushing his chest and the hardness of him against my belly. Clutching him tightly around the waist with my thighs, I took him deep inside me where I was open and ready and sweet as honey.

"I love you, Ursula," he told me later, as we spooned, his chest pressed into my back and his nose into my neck, where he inhaled the scent of my hair which, released of its tight confines, rippled like a dark shadow across the pillow. "Whatever happens to us in this life, always remember that."

I turned onto my back and, putting up a hand, stroked his face, feeling the stubble on his chin rasp against my palm. "I love you too," I told him. "Oh Gregory, I love you too."

I pulled myself up onto my elbows and, resting my head on my palm, gazed down the full length of his slim body — at his muscular chest, his manhood curled up now like the cat that slept on the hearth, at his long lithe legs. I played with the hairs on his chest, my fingers stroking and gently pulling, when I noticed a small white edged mark just above his left nipple.

"What is this, Gregory?" I asked him, frowning, tracing the outline of the shape with my finger.

Gazing down, he said, "Ah, the crescent moon. That, my dear Ursula, is a scar from when I had the smallpox many years ago. I was lucky—I was a survivor."

"Yes, it does indeed look like a crescent moon," I said softly as I bent over him, my hair trailing on his face, and kissed the mark tenderly, my tongue licking it, tasting it. He pulled me closer to him and kissed my lips, and his manhood rose up to greet me. So full of lust and passion, we devoured each other again.

Chapter Eleven

Claire went back to London and Sarah returned to work, her shingles all cleared up and having been given a clean bill of health by the doctor. I gazed at her at work, peering into her office, watching her sitting at the computer typing up letters and conveyances and legal charges, all the while knowing that she led a double life. Her first as Sarah Miller, Legal Secretary to Stuart Rhodes, Reynolds and Rhodes, Solicitors, and the second one as Elizabeth the First, Queen of England. Wow. What more could I say?

I watched Max too. Max, who also led two lives — or so he said — his first as Max Reynolds, Founder of Reynolds & Rhodes Solicitors, and his second as Gregory Walsh, gardener to Sir Richard Pole and Margaret Pole. I still shook my head at this, although a niggling memory of meeting him at the ruin still lingered in my mind. The day I went to confront him about this, to ask him what had happened, I found myself with Gregory in his tiny cottage in the grounds of Warblington Manor, and the thought of what we did together in his soft double bed in his bedchamber beneath the eaves still made me blush.

I didn't think I would, but I was amazed at how much I

missed Claire. Although she texted me on a regular basis, and we had spoken a few times since she went back to London to set up home with her partner, Laura, I wished that she was still in Havant working in Smith & Vosper, and buying my lunch in Wetherspoons.

Now that I knew she was gay, the jealousy that I'd felt at seeing her with Max had completely gone. That little green imp that used to sit on my shoulder whispering evil thoughts into my ear had disappeared. Why had I felt that way, though? Why was I envious of her relationship with Max? I supposed it would always remain a mystery, although I really did think that Max's resemblance to Gregory had a huge bearing on it.

My little Mini Daphne ground to a halt in front of Mum and Dad's house in Cosham, a three-bedroom semi-detached with a large garden front and back — the house where I was born and the house I'd grown up in. I walked along the drive past Dad's old Rover with its cracked leather seats, and giving the back door a little tap, walked straight in. The kitchen smelled like the local Indian takeaway, and Mum was standing at the cooker stirring some sort of bright red concoction with a wooden spoon.

She stopped what she was doing and, wiping her hands on a tea towel, pulled me into a warm hug, reminding me suddenly of Margaret Pole. I looked at her, temporarily confused because she wasn't wearing a long heavy gown and a little peaked hood on her head, but a pair of jeans and a blue and white striped shirt, a pair of green pom pom slippers on her feet.

"Hannah, darling, how are you?"

"I'm fine, Mum. Mmm, looks good," I said as I peered into the pan on the stove. "Is this our tea?"

My stomach rumbled alarmingly, prompting Mum to

say, "Yes, it's curry," giving it another quick stir. "A spicy chicken curry, with rice and poppadoms and onion chutney salad. I hope you like it."

"Ooh, get you," I said, and then, "I'm pretty sure I will."

She grinned at me before saying, "I'm not sure if your dad will. He seems to think that anything spicy is weird."

"What? Who's talking about me?" said a voice, and Dad appeared in the kitchen wearing his old man's uniform—as mum called it—of baggy jeans with an open necked shirt, a V-necked vest—of which he had many, in all different colors—over the top. Straight away he enveloped me in a hug before pulling back, his hands on my shoulders, frowning and studying my face intently. "Hmm, what's wrong with you? You look like a bulldog chewing a wasp."

"Thanks, Dad," I said, thinking no matter how much I bothered about my appearance Dad would always make some sort of silly comment, making me feel that all my effort had been wasted.

"Don't take offense," he said. "You just look tired, that's all."

A fleeting thought passed through my mind that, yes, I probably did look tired after all I'd been through the past few months, but there was no way that I could tell Dad about that. I couldn't tell him that I'd had a traumatic birth experience where I'd almost died, and then lost my baby Henry to smallpox. After which King Henry the Eighth of England had found me a husband, who I was assured would be a good husband and that it would be an excellent match. But he beat me and was unfaithful, not with a woman, as I'd expected, but with a man who was a particular favorite at King Henry's court.

And to top it all I then experienced some very strenuous

love making with Gregory Walsh, the gardener to my mother and father, Sir Richard Pole and Margaret Pole. How much more could a girl take, Dad?

"Leave her alone," said Mum. "She looks lovely as always. This curry is ready, so both of you — and you, Ryan...." My little brother sauntered into the kitchen. "Go and sit at the table and I'll bring it in."

"Have you heard from Claire?" asked Dad, as he helped himself to a good-sized spoonful of the curry.

I nodded. "Yes, we text regularly, and speak sometimes."

"Good God, Marjorie," he said as he took a tiny taste. "This is really spicy." He did some sort of heavy panting, his lips in an O shape as if he were in labor.

"Calm down, Bill," replied Mum. She shook her head and gave a great heartfelt sigh.

"It's well good," said Ryan, piling his plate high.

"I couldn't believe it when she told us she was setting up home with a woman," said Dad, nibbling at a poppadum. "Came as a bit of a surprise, that did, I can tell you." He put a hand to his heart and raised his eyes to the ceiling.

I stopped eating, my fork in midair, and gaped at him. "She told you that?"

"Yes, of course she did," said Mum and Dad in unison.

"She's well pretty," pointed out Ryan.

"Who's pretty?" I asked. "Claire?" I poked absent mindedly at the onion chutney salad with a fork. I could hardly believe this conversation.

"No. Laura, Claire's girlfriend." Ryan spooned curry and rice into his mouth like there was no tomorrow.

"Have you met her?" I asked in confusion, and also jealous that I hadn't been invited to meet her too.

"No," Ryan replied. "Claire sent me a picture on Facebook.

She looks a bit like Halle Berry. You know, that actress."

"Really? So she's dark then?" I could just imagine her and Claire together, the light side and the dark side, milk chocolate and dark chocolate, the good and the bad, but definitely not the ugly.

Mum nodded and said, "Yes, she's got short hair and she's dark."

"Dark hair?"

"For God's sake," boomed Dad. "She's got black hair and black skin."

"No, not black," pointed out Ryan. "Halle Berry hasn't got black skin."

"Well, no, she hasn't," agreed Dad sarcastically, glaring at Ryan. "But then again, Claire's girlfriend isn't Halle Berry, is she?"

"Actually," butted in Mum, who was picking and poking at her curry with a fork. "She looks a lot like Megan Markle." Three pairs of wide-open eyes stared at her in amazement.

After such a confusing conversation, I was relieved when we retired to the sitting room and Mum handed me a glass of sherry which, after taking a healthy slug to calm my nerves, I put on the small coffee table.

"Sit there, Hannah," Mum said, pointing to the armchair nearest to the fireplace. "You can put that book on the floor."

I glanced at the book as I picked it up. It was always interesting to see what Mum was reading. She was a real proper bookworm, and must get through at least ten books a week. To my total astonishment, the book was called, *The Life and Times of Margaret Pole*. I almost dropped it in shock.

Margaret Pole? I thought, flicking through the book and looking at the pictures, immediately recognizing her, my mother, the lady that I'd met often but in a different time, a different century. The lady that had held my hand tightly through the birth of my baby. The lady that used my nickname of Little Bear. The lady who kept my secrets, and the lady that I'd seen on her death day being hacked to pieces by a bloody axe. I sat down heavily on the settee, feeling short of breath and panting as if in labor, as Dad had earlier when tasting the spicy curry.

Thankfully nobody seemed to notice, and I asked Mum quite calmly, "What's with this book, Mum?"

"Ooh, it's brilliant," she said. "It's all about Margaret Pole. Have you heard of her?"

"Well, yes, I have. But —"

"Really interesting local history, you know, Hannah. And also, I think there may be some sort of connection between their family and ours."

"A connection?" I asked, hardly able to believe my ears. "What connection?"

"I've got to do a bit more research, but there were Palmers at King Henry's court — one of them a musician, I think."

What was Henry Stafford's lover called? Oh my God yes, William Palmer. Why hadn't I noticed that before? Did that mean that I could be related to my husband's boyfriend? Wow.

"Also," Mum went on, "The connection with Henry the Eighth is fascinating, and —"

Whatever else Mum was going to say was lost in the ether, as all of a sudden my phone beeped and a text flashed up. Peering closely, I saw it was a message from, of all people, Max.

Hi Hannah. I'm outside your mum and dad's, saw your car. Have you got time for a quick chat?

Before I could respond to the text, Ryan shouted out,

"Hannah, that boss man of yours is coming down the garden path."

I peered from between the curtains and sure enough, there he was, Max Reynolds, trying to peer through the obscure glass window set into the front door before realizing that he was wasting his time and using the brass knocker to give a sharp rat tat tat.

A beam of sunshine pooled on the carpet as I pulled the door open and we came face to face. He looked cool and casual as usual, dressed in a smart dark suit and white shirt, an overcoat hanging open over the top. He'd obviously just come from work.

"Hi, did you get my message?"

"Yes, but only just," I replied. "God Max, you could have given me time to reply."

"Yeah, but.... Well, we need to talk, Hannah. Do you fancy a coffee, or a beer?"

"Okay then. Will have to be a coffee; I've just had sherry with Mum and Dad." And then, nodding towards my car, I said, "I'm driving."

"No problem. There's a great little cafe bar in Cosham town center. Do you fancy a walk?"

I beckoned him in and Max stepped into the sitting room where Mum and Dad sat watching the television. Dad had his arms crossed over his chest and a look of horror on his face as he watched a very bloody operation on a cute Labradoodle puppy. It had to be the *Super Vet* program. Ryan had disappeared into his bedroom, and was no doubt scrolling through Facebook and admiring pictures of Claire's gorgeous new girlfriend.

The faint drone of Max's voice sounded from the sitting room as he made conversation with my parents, so I left him there and went into the kitchen to collect my bag and coat. Suddenly feeling the need for the loo, I dashed upstairs, taking the steps two at a time—I didn't want to keep the big boss waiting—but when I got up there, everything looked so different.

The landing was twice the size, and square, not long and thin as it always had been. When I peered around the toilet door, it wasn't a toilet any longer, but a dressing room. A massive wooden chest stood along one wall next to a dressing table and stool, and a huge stand-alone mirror with a gilded beveled edge took pride of place in the middle of the room.

A rotund maid dressed in a black dress with a white frilly apron tied over the top was busily searching through the chest, both arms deep within the voluminous folds of brightly colored gowns and undergarments. With a flourish she pulled out a sky-blue garter.

My mother, Margaret Pole, appeared at my side. "Ursula, Little Bear, come, let us get you ready. Why do you tarry? It is your wedding day." She smiled broadly, and I noticed that she held a beautiful white gown that drooped over her arm like the neck of a swan, and with a sinking heart I realized that I was Ursula Pole again, and today would be the day that I married Henry Stafford, 1st Baron Stafford, son of the 3rd Duke of Buckingham.

Chapter Twelve

It was April, the fourth month of the year, yet not the first day, the Fool's Day, but the second day, my wedding day, and from the window, through the warm sun drenched panes, I saw daffodils, clusters of bright yellow and cream daffodils nodding and swaying in the chilly spring breeze like shy ladies hanging their golden heads. Their brightness dazzled me and my eyes hurt. They stung, they watered until they were red rimmed and I looked as if I'd been weeping.

Standing in front of the mirror, the tall oblong mirror with gilded beveled edges, I stared at my image and my image stared back at me. I raise my hand and my image raised its hand. I touched my hair and my image touched its hair. We were as one, a carbon copy—we were twins. We had the same dark eyes flecked with splinters of gold, and our hair, adorned with a circle of wild flowers, was long and loose on our shoulders and down our backs as a symbol of purity.

Our wedding dress was white interwoven with a silver thread, and the skirt, as wide as a puffy meringue, flared over our hips, stomach, and thighs like a bell, a sweet melodic chiming bell that, as we moved, rustled and whispered along the floor like voices murmuring secrets. The sleeves were full

119

and tapered at the wrist, and the whole gown was alive with sparkling emeralds and rubies.

"Something old," muttered my mother, Margaret Pole, as she helped me into an old lacy petticoat that was concealed, like a child playing hide and seek, beneath the full skirt of my wedding gown. "Something new," as I pulled on new flesh colored stockings. "Something borrowed," as my mother, Margaret Pole, hung her very own golden locket around my neck, and "Something blue" as the garter, blue as the sky on a hot summer day, encircled my slim thigh.

"You are ready," said my mother as she stood back to inspect me and then nodded with satisfaction. "You are fair as a summer day, my dear, worthy of any man." My mother's ladies bowed their heads as I walked past with my father, Sir Richard Pole, who held my arm tightly as we stepped out into the spring sunshine and took the short walk along the petal-strewn path from Warblington Manor to St. Thomas à Becket Church.

Fluffy white clouds floated slowly in the blue sky, and the leaves on the trees shone so brightly they hurt my eyes. A piper playing *Greensleeves* danced ahead. Crowds lined the path, shouting and cheering, and I bowed my head so my face could not be seen. My bridesmaids' blue gowns haunted my vision as they pursued me along the aisle and to the altar, where Henry Stafford awaited me, the expression on his face both malicious and triumphant.

"Hannah? Hannah?" It was Max's voice; or was it Gregory's? My head was swimming and, hearing footsteps on the stairs, I quickly put my hands over my eyes and shook my head, hoping the dizziness would go away. Opening them slowly and carefully, I saw that I was no longer in the dressing room but the toilet, and I was wearing the black trousers and red blouse that I wore for work that day. My beautiful wedding gown had vanished into another time and another place, as had Ursula Pole.

Max called again and I shouted out, "Okay, I'm coming — two minutes."

I quickly checked my reflection in the mirror, Hannah's reflection, before running downstairs to meet him.

~*~

Mooch Cafe Bar on Cosham High Street was fairly busy when Max and I eventually got there, but it was nearing the weekend and most people would probably be enjoying that Friday feeling. As we walked Max had a bit of a dig at me about what I'd been doing all that time upstairs at Mum and Dad's. He gazed at me for some time, his eyes narrowed. "A trip back in time eh, Ursula — Little Bear?" he said with particular emphasis on the name Ursula, before opening the door of the cafe and ushering me in ahead of him.

"My name's Hannah," I retorted as we went in and found a table for two by the window. "And anyway, it's not something to be ridiculed...Max. And how did you know about Ursula's nickname?"

"I'm not ridiculing it, and of course I know Ursula's nickname," he replied casually as he studied the drinks menu, opting for a coffee latte, and I a hot chocolate with the whole works of cream and a flake. At that moment in time I didn't care about steps and diet.

"What do you want to talk about, Max?" I asked him as I licked cream from a long silver spoon and then dunked the flake into the hot chocolate until it began to melt.

Taking a sip of coffee, he shook his head as he watched my antics with the hot chocolate, commenting that I was just like a child before leaning forward his elbows on the table and saying, "I want you to believe me when I tell you that I am Gregory Walsh."

"Oh, so that's what all this is about? Max, for God's sake, it's just not possible."

"What do you mean?" he asked, taken aback. "You're Ursula Pole, aren't you? How can you say that what happens to you is possible, but not what happens to me?"

"That's different," I said lamely.

He licked froth from his lips before shaking his head and saying, "No it isn't."

I tried not to look at him while he was licking his lips, as it sent a not unpleasant shiver down my spine, so I gazed around at our surroundings, thinking what a nice trendy place it was. Not just a coffee bar, but a night out sort of bar as well, as they served wine and spirits as well as coffee and light snacks. The lighting was low, and the tables, made of blonde wood, were round, like little mushrooms had sprung up everywhere, and there were big squashy pouffes to sit on. Music played softly, some sort of Latin American stuff, which was really good.

Vintage posters adorned the cream and beige walls, and skinny candles in wine bottles flickered on the tables and pretty pink fairy lights twinkled around the bar. I noticed that people drank beer and sipped at red wine from massive balloon glasses. Good God, it was only just after six o'clock.

All the customers looked really cool and stylish—ripped jeans, tattoos, pierced noses and ears. I felt positively dowdy compared to them having no tattoos or piercings whatsoever. Just imagine if I had one and went back as Ursula Pole. I didn't think she would look good with a tattoo. It was surprising, though, that King Henry hadn't made a rule that everybody had to have a tattoo of the royal standard on their shoulder or their ankle, or "off with their head." Ha, how funny that would be.

"Hannah, you're miles away? What are you thinking about?"

I came back to the present time and to Max, and said, "Actually, Max, I was thinking about Ursula Pole and how a tattoo wouldn't look good on her. So I'm glad I don't have any."

He laughed so loudly that a lot of the customers looked around and grinned, and just for a moment, for a split second, I wished that Max and I were a couple and were out together drinking red wine and having a good time. Then, as quickly as it had come, the feeling went away, and all I could see was his procession of Barbie dolls that had come and gone right in front of my eyes in such a short space of time.

"Seriously, Hannah, as Gregory I've been with you many times, and mostly in times of crisis; it should be so obvious to you now. Look at what happened when I saw you at the ruin and we put our hands on the stones together." I must have looked blank, because he said, "Surely you remember that – it was only a few weeks ago."

"I'm not sure," I muttered as I took a sip of hot chocolate.

"We went back in time again after that, and you came to my cottage, well, Gregory's cottage," he whispered. "We ended up in the sack, Hannah."

I looked up abruptly. "The sack?"

"I mean we went to bed for the first time. We made love. Gregory and Ursula love each other, Hannah. If they were of the same station and birth, they would probably be married."

"Yes, Gregory and Ursula for sure – but not Max and Hannah," I said quietly.

"Yeah. Well...." He thoughtfully stirred his coffee with

123

a spoon and then looked up at me, sending shivers down my spine again—he looked so much like Gregory. "There's something between us though, isn't there, Hannah?"

"No," I said calmly, although my heart was thumping like a crazy thing. "Boss and personal assistant, Max. As you said before, it wouldn't work."

A group of people came chattering through the doorway, drowning out our conversation. When it quietened down again Max said, "You came to me through the deep snow when you were upset about baby Henry's death, and when your mother told you that King Henry had found you a husband. And do you remember the day the king arrived unannounced at Warblington Manor?"

I nodded slowly as I thought back to that lovely summer day when Gregory and I had embraced in the gardens of Warblington Manor, and a fanfare had sounded out of nowhere heralding the arrival of King Henry. I didn't think we'd been seen hiding beneath the spreading branches of the trees, but we had, by my mother, Margaret Pole, who kept my secret to the end—to her bitter, gruesome end.

All the things that Max was saying to me were true, perfectly true. But oh God, it couldn't be, it just couldn't be that Max was Gregory. And if I was in love with Gregory, then did it mean that I was in love with Max too?

"You always come to me, Hannah. You know who I am, please don't deny it."

He leaned in closer and took my hands in his. Blushing, I averted my gaze and looked out of the window instead. I watched as people, tired from working all day, got slowly off the bus at the stop opposite. A boy zoomed past on a skateboard and a couple of girls jogged by, chatting animatedly. Then a little old lady shuffled along holding a canvas shopping bag, the words Do More Yoga printed on its side.

"I know what will clinch it," said Max suddenly. "I have proof." He started to loosen his tie and unbutton his shirt.

"Whoa, Max, what are you doing?" I held up my hand like a traffic cop. "Not here." I glanced around to see the girl serving drinks at the bar stop momentarily to see what was going on. Her eyes almost popped out of her head as she ogled Max's bare chest, lager foaming in a golden stream over the top of the pint glass she was filling.

Grinning and still unbuttoning his shirt in what could only be called a slow and erotic manner, he said triumphantly, "The crescent moon, Hannah. Look." As he pulled his shirt wide open, there it was, the tiny crescent moon, the shape that I'd seen so recently just below the left nipple on the sexy bare chest of Gregory Walsh.

Totally lost for words, I stared at Max's chest, even, in shock, rubbing my finger over the tiny shape that nestled amongst the slight hairs around his nipple. How could it be? Now this really was impossible.

"Well, what do you say now?"

"No." A sudden panic took hold of me and, pushing back my chair and standing up, I said, "No, Max. I still don't believe you. It just can't be true."

The girl behind the bar, pouring wine now, looked disappointed as Max buttoned up his shirt and tightened his tie before standing up and, bewildered, said, "Hannah...?"

Without a backward glance, I dashed out of the door of the Mooch Cafe Bar, and ran frantically down the road, my heels clattering on the pavement as if I really was being pursued by the Fitbit Police.

Chapter Thirteen

I gazed out of the sitting room window of Warblington Manor at the gardens beyond. It was October and the leaves on the trees were turning, the colors of red, yellow, and gold magnificent against the hard bright blue of the sky. A fresh breeze whipped at the trees' bony branches until they bent and swayed like wayward string puppets. In the distance I saw a black and white figure hunched over the flower borders, furiously digging, weeding, and planting. He had his back to me so could not see my hungry longing gaze, for I had not been alone with Gregory Walsh for some time now. Although, I smiled wryly, my large belly may say otherwise.

Absentmindedly I stroked the huge mound, feeling the baby curled inside like a tiny question mark shift a little, and a fleeting feeling of rising bubbles made my heartbeat quicken. I smiled to myself, unsure if it was my time yet, but a vague needling in my lower back pained me, reminding me of the traumatic labor to beget baby Henry. Such a long time ago, almost six years, but these things were not easily forgotten.

"A penny for them, Little Bear?"

I turned around to see my father, Sir Richard Pole, sitting elegantly in an armchair pulled up close to a fire that crackled bright orange and red in the grate. He had an open book in his hand, into which he placed a slice of leather he used as a bookmark before putting the book on the round occasional table at his side. Casually he crossed one knee over the other and, reaching for his enamel snuff box, took a tiny pinch between his finger and thumb and inhaled deeply.

"The baby did move, Father," I told him. "And that feeling always makes me smile."

I gave a tiny curtsey and sat down next to my mother, Margaret Pole, who was sitting on a settee, her voluminous skirts spread around her. She was sewing a sampler that was changing like magic day by day into a picture of Warblington Manor and its beautiful gardens. I gazed in wonder at her artistry; such tiny delicate stitches in brown and umber that shaped the walls of the house, the green that portrayed the grass, and the blue the sky. Flower buds in mouth-watering shades of red and pink and lemon were conjured up like sleight of hand against the dark silk background.

Putting her work aside for a moment, she placed her hands carefully on my mound and closed her eyes. "Why yes, Ursula, I feel her too. Is that a foot or is that a hand?"

I giggled as I asked, "Her? Will we welcome a female this time do you think, Mother?"

"Oh, my dear, I will not prophesy, not even here amongst us three." My mother lowered her voice and gazed around, as if somebody was there, watching from the shadowy corners of the sitting room. "It is more than my life is worth to be talking of such things. Although it could be that your mound is the right shape for a girl child."

"Hmm," said my father softly, as if to himself. "Witchcraft can be hard to prove. But if it were known that you even guessed at a female and a female it was, there would be much trouble for you." He nodded his head knowingly, and for good measure took a much larger pinch from his little enamel snuff box and breathed in heartily.

The door opened and my husband, Henry Stafford, sauntered into the room. I knew not where he had been, but suspected that William Palmer did. I also did not know if my mother and father knew of his sexual preferences, but sometimes suspected that my mother did if only by the glint in her eyes as she witnessed, dandy that he was, his limp wristed ways and girlish speech. She must have wondered both times how I had come to be pregnant by him. All I could say was that it was a disappointing and loveless act for both of us. Nothing at all could compare that hurried fumbling with the leisurely sexual dance that occurred between myself and my lover. But if that was how it must be, then so it must stay. I had no choice in the matter.

A sudden longing for Gregory overcame me as Henry sashayed to my side and, picking up my hand which lay rigidly across my bump, pecked at it with thin cold lips. I could not help but compare them to Gregory's, which were as full and lush as tender spring grass.

"My dear Ursula," he crooned. "How are you today, wife?"

Giving a tiny bow of my head, I said, "Quite well thank you, husband. Although," and here I turned to my mother, "I have a needling pain here in my back." I sat forward and put both hands to my sacrum. "As I did when baby Henry started to come."

Alarmed, my mother said softly as she gently felt my mound with her hands, "The babe is almost fully grown. Perhaps it is time, although I didn't think so yet. Perhaps the midwife should come." And then almost to herself, she continued, "It is fortunate that we are prepared and the birthing room is ready." She looked to my father in a panic. "Perhaps we should call Mrs. Dawes."

My father, stunned and obviously going to be of little use, gave a small nod of his head as my mother hurried from the room to ask the maid to fetch the midwife. Henry made to sit beside me, but the needling pain intensified and, as I tried to stand, I felt a breaking high up between my legs. Liquid, like a tap turned on full, gushed down my thighs and pooled around my feet in their soft green slippers.

In a panic my father, together with Henry, sprang up and held my arms to steady me, but only succeeded in slipping and sliding like skaters on the oily fluid that was spreading over the stone flagged floor. With great relief I saw my mother hurry back into the room, bringing the good news that Mrs. Dawes was on her way. So, whimpering like a wounded animal and feeling so very, very afraid, I let her lead me gently to the birthing room.

~*~

Max's office was shadowy and dim and, after such promising sunshine this morning, I was surprised to find that I had to flick the lights on as I went in. Peering from the tiny window, I saw that rain now fell from the clouds in long silver rods, soaking into the earth that had become dry and crumbly during the warmer weather.

Water in tiny rivers ran down the old Havant Road and a car drove past, tires hissing, and splashing a pedestrian who battled with an umbrella in the squally wind. A sudden shiver ran down my spine and, hunching my shoulders to my ears, I wrapped my chilly arms, clad in only thin silky sleeves, around my waist.

My mind raced madly with thoughts of Ursula Pole and

her impending labor. God help her if it was as bad as with baby Henry. According to Wikipedia, Margaret Pole, had been correct in her assumption that it would be a girl child this time. A girl who would go by the name of Dorothy, and who would rise very high and become an influential lady at the court of Elizabeth I, Queen of England. Did Margaret's prophecy have anything to do with her downfall and eventual execution? Had somebody overheard their conversation that day in the sitting room, Henry Stafford for example, and given birth, so to speak, to the accusation of witchcraft as well as treason?

Trying desperately to put it out of my mind and bring my attention to Max's filing, I began to flick purposefully through the buff files, sorting them into piles and then putting them in alphabetical order. Max was in court for the next couple of days, and had left strict instructions for me in a bulleted note form, the most important request being to clear the filing. Rain pattered against the window and a ghostly wind moaned, reminding me even more of Ursula Pole, who even now, albeit centuries before, could be writhing and panting on her bloody child bed.

There was a tiny tap and Sarah peeked around the office door, carrying two steaming mugs of coffee on a little round tray.

"Hey, Hannah, are you okay?"

"Sarah. Yes, of course, come in. Ooh coffee, thanks."

She put both mugs on Max's desk. "Hey, I thought you might fancy a warm drink. It's gone really cold." She hunched her shoulders, "And as well as that I need a file—Mr. and Mrs. Luckhurst? Cordelia and Mark?"

I went to the filing cabinet and, after having a quick flick through, pulled out a file. "Cordelia Luckhurst," I said. "Yes, here it is. What a name, eh?"

Sarah giggled and said, "Hey, yes, it certainly is." She sipped from her mug and, after taking the file from me, put it on the desk. "Hey, is everything all right with you? I feel as if we haven't chatted for a while, even at home."

"Yeah I know. You'd think we'd see each other all the time because we live in the same house, but it doesn't work like that, does it?" I drank from my mug and said, "Umm, just what I needed."

Sarah smiled and said, "Hey, no, it doesn't. We're both so busy, and I've been at Neil's quite a bit. I don't think I've talked to you properly since I came back to work. How's Claire since she went back to London?"

"Claire's fine," I told her.

"She disappeared pretty quickly again, didn't she? I think Stuart wanted to get her a leaving present, but one minute she was there, the next gone."

"Well, yes, I suppose she did. You do know why she went back, don't you?"

"Hey, well, not really. But I suspect it involves a man."

"Um no, not really. Actually, Sarah, it involves a woman."

Sarah looked completely blank, so I carried on speaking and filled her in on all the juicy details about Claire's lover, Laura.

Finally Sarah found her voice and said, "Hey, good God. What did your mum and dad say?"

"They're okay with it, although I think it shook Dad up a bit." I had a vivid image of Dad putting his hand to his heart after almost choking on the spicy chicken curry.

"Hey, well, I can't top that for news." We both giggled. "Anything to tell me about events in your other life as Ursula Pole?"

"Well, events in the 1500s are pretty hard to come to terms with, and definitely more gruesome than my life here," I joked. Then I said more seriously, "Yeah, well, you know about baby Henry and the execution of my mother, Margaret Pole, which was totally awful and upsetting. Oh, this will be of particular interest to you, because at my last visit Ursula went into labor with her second child, Dorothy—"

Sarah butted in, excited. "Oh my God. Dorothy Stafford, who grows up to be mistress of the robes to Queen Elizabeth I. She stayed Dorothy Stafford when she married William Stafford, who, incidentally, was married to Anne Boleyn's sister, Mary until she died. Did you know that, Hannah?"

"No, I didn't. Wow. How complicated their lives were— talk about intermingled. What was Dorothy like, Sarah?"

"Hey, she was lovely. A great lady, who came to be a great friend and ally to me in my guise of Elizabeth the First." She nodded her head slowly.

"Wow, that's amazing. Actually though, Sarah, I know I'm changing the subject in a way, but I'd like to talk to you about Max."

"Max?"

"Yeah, Max. He came looking for me at my mum and dad's—said he wanted to talk to me about his other life as Gregory Walsh. I don't believe him at all, Sarah. I think he's spinning a tale and making fun of me." Sarah remained ominously silent and sipped her coffee, so I carried on talking. "The weird thing, though, is that he has the exact same mark on him that Gregory Walsh has—a tiny crescent moon shape. Apparently it's a smallpox scar, on his chest just below his left nipple. It's also in the exact same spot as the one Gregory has. I don't understand it. It's pretty scary really—spooks me out. And he also knows Ursula's nickname, Little Bear, and only her family ever used that."

I then relayed the whole story about Max pulling open his shirt in the Mooch Cafe bar to show me the scar as being proof that he was telling the truth. Sarah laughed and shook her head, saying how typical that was of Max, but still annoyingly didn't make a comment.

"You're very quiet, Sarah," I said. "Come on—is there something I need to know?"

She took a deep breath and said, "Hey, actually, Hannah, Max isn't spinning you a tale or making fun of you. It's true, he is Gregory Walsh. He talked to me all about it when it first began happening to him, and I told him about my experiences too."

My legs felt shaky, so I sat down on Max's leather swivel chair and Sarah followed suit by sitting on the chair that I usually sat on opposite Max. I noticed that at last it had stopped raining and the wind had died down, and the sun, just a faint glimmer, was trying to come out from between grey clouds. The pavements sparkled and glittered in the weak sunlight, and cars swished by, their headlights shining in the gloom.

"God, Sarah, are you sure?"

"Hey, absolutely. Do you remember when you asked me if I'd confided in anybody about my experiences, and I told you I'd been to a lady who did past life regression?"

"Yes, you gave me a card just in case I wanted to go to her."

"Hey, yes, that's right. Well, Max went to her too, and there's no doubt about it, Hannah. Max is Gregory Walsh. Anyway...." She suddenly changed the subject. "How do you know that Gregory has a crescent shaped scar on his chest below his left nipple? That seems rather intimate—a bit sort of *Lady Chatterley's Lover*." She looked disapproving, a frown creasing her forehead, although her beautiful almond shaped eyes glittered with mirth.

Heat suffused my face as an image of Gregory Walsh lying naked on his bed under the eaves came to mind, and I grinned at her, my lips involuntarily turning up in a smile. "Well, let's just say that we became very close one time when I visited him at his cottage. I had an excuse—I was upset because the king had found me a husband, who turned out to be Henry Stafford."

"Hey, Henry Stafford?" queried Sarah.

"Yes," I said, then remembered what Gregory had told me. "A man who is a man but isn't a man."

"Hey, I see. So you got your loving from Gregory instead? And I suppose you're thinking that if you made love to Gregory, that really you've also made love to Max?"

"Oh good God, no," I replied, my heart thumping hard. "That can't be right. Max is my boss. And, anyway, I'm not Max's type. I'm too dark, too short, and too chubby."

"Hey, that's got nothing to do with it, Hannah, not your looks or the fact that he's your boss. If it happened with Gregory and Gregory is Max.... Well, it happened then, okay? It looks to me like Max is your soul mate, and I think you should face up to that and go and see him, and have a proper talk."

I drank down the last of my coffee, the dregs tasting bitter in my mouth, and gazing straight at her I said, "I don't know, Sarah. I think it might be better if I get another job, or maybe a transfer to another branch of Reynolds & Rhodes. I just don't think I can work with Max anymore."

Sarah looked upset and shook her head vehemently. "Hey, don't make any hasty decisions, Hannah. Think about it for a while, please. I don't think that Max would want you to go."

"Hmm, I'm not sure about that," I replied. "But okay, I'll wait and see what happens. I won't speak to Max just yet. I'll choose my time carefully."

Chapter Fourteen

I paced my bedchamber backwards and forwards, backwards and forwards, my soft embroidered slippers shushing on the sweet scented rushes that covered the bumpy old floorboards, my hands twined together so tightly that my knuckles shone white. I didn't know what to do with myself. My grief was so deep and so palpable that I suspected I may never recover.

I had thought that the death of baby Henry was hard to bear, and sadly, the recent death of my father. But the execution of my mother, Margaret Pole, had rendered me helpless. My grief ate away at me, just as the worms and the insects devoured my mother's flesh as she lay in the mud and dust of the earth. The thought of her not being buried whole made me wring my hands with a terrible misery. What havoc King Henry had wrought since he took the throne.

Standing at the large bay window, I saw that once again it was a fine day. Every day had been a beautiful sunny day since my mother died — or should I say since my mother was murdered. I'd never seen the sky so blue, the grass so green, the flowers so bright. It was as if Mother Nature was mocking me, laughing at me, giving the illusion that all was well when it was not. I was trapped in a dark, suffocating tunnel of grief, with no hope of escape. There was no hope. Not anymore.

I heard high pitched laughter like the tinkling of bells, and saw that my children played in the beautiful gardens of Warblington Manor. I had managed to stay there for now in my childhood home, much to my husband's disgust, but I had a terrible fear that now my mother was no longer there, the house, which was a gift to her from King Henry, would be seized, and where would we go then? Would we go back to London to Henry's family? My heart ached at the thought of leaving Warblington.

I watched my daughter, my Dorothy, my heart, who was but fifteen years old now, the very age I was when I married Henry Stafford. I hoped that a better husband would be chosen for her, a loving husband, a man like Gregory Walsh, from whom she would receive kisses and hugs and joy. I vowed that I would have a say in the matter regardless of how difficult that may be.

I watched my boys in the garden too. Henry, reminding me of the first Henry, who had died such a long time ago, and Thomas and Edward. Oh, and there was Richard too, and Walter. All of them so young and so vibrant and so free. I had many children, all of whom had given my mother, Margaret Pole, such pleasure. For this I was glad, for sometimes guilt at not being able to prevent her death overcame me, and how I stifled my screams I did not know.

My husband, Henry Stafford, grumbled and whined, and told me that my mother should never have prophesied about the baby that I carried in my belly, and that her gossip about Queen Anne had angered King Henry.

"How did she know you carried a girl?" he hissed at me time and time again. "It was witchcraft," he whispered close to my ear. "It was witchcraft, Ursula, my dear wife, and she has paid the price."

"That was idle talk only," I said hysterically. "A mere guess. And as for gossip about Queen Anne, it was my brother's gossip, not my mother's."

My stomach felt tight as a drum beneath the voluminous folds of my gown, and the suspicion that I may be pregnant again made me cup my rounded belly hard with my hands. I had lost track of my courses, and thought that perhaps it was grief that had made the secret place between my legs so dry and unresisting. But then again, it had never been anything else for my husband, Henry Stafford. Gregory was the only man that could ever make sweet juices run so freely from a body that became supple and pliant at his touch.

Breathless with misery and with an urge for Gregory, I ran from my bedchamber, my gown floating behind me like the sail of a ship and my headdress swaying as I moved. I was careful to leave from the back door so I would not be seen by my children, who played at the front of the house. The heat was thick and sludgy as glue as I tried to walk through it, and sweat broke out under my arms and between my breasts. It trickled from beneath my headdress and into my eyes, where it stung so badly I was almost blinded.

The cottage, Gregory's cottage, stood empty and still when finally I arrived, the door firmly closed and latched and the windows a terrifying blank. No smoke trailed from the chimney, and in the garden no chickens clucked and scratched at the ground with clawed feet. I peered in the windows and saw nothing but empty rooms. No fire burned in the grate, and no black cat, shiny as a lump of coal, was curled on the hearth.

Gregory was not there. I banged on the door with my fists

until they blossomed into ripe yellow, green, and blue bruises, but there was no answer, no opening swing of the door and Gregory's smiling face. I sank to my knees in the dust and the dirt, my beautiful mourning gown spreading around me like a pool of dark water and my hands covering my face. How could I bear this as well as everything else? How could I live this life now that Gregory had gone?

~*~

I spent the evening reading about Ursula Pole on Wikipedia, and wondered yet again how she had managed to live so long with all that she had gone through — the fourteen pregnancies, the death of her baby, and the execution of her mother. Even one of her brothers had been executed. I supposed that was what life was like then, and Ursula's was barely different from anybody else's.

I googled Gregory Walsh desperately, but could still find no trace of him. I was searching for clues as to why he would disappear without telling Ursula where he was going. I felt sure that he would have tried somehow to get word to her. Smiling to myself, I realized that getting a message to somebody in those days wasn't easy. How did they manage without a telephone, without text messages and emails? It wasn't as though Gregory could have just left her a note under the mat. He would have had to find a boy to take her a message, and paid him a penny or whatever the going rate was in those days. Now why hadn't he done that?

I had a feeling that the whole thing was tied up with the dreaded Henry Stafford. Perhaps he had found out about Ursula's affair and sought revenge on Gregory. The thought of any harm coming to Gregory was hard to bear, and the feeling that I would never see him again stayed with me for the rest of the evening, an evening where alone for once, as Sarah was staying with Neil, I also did some good hard thinking about my dilemma with Max.

It was pretty obvious now that I would have to speak to him in light of what Sarah had told me about Max really and truly being Gregory Walsh. A sudden thought occurred to me; Max would be able to tell me why Gregory had disappeared without a word. Yes, why didn't I think of that before? If anybody could tell me, it had to be Max. If, of course, he was who he said he was. And according to Sarah, he was Gregory without a doubt.

I still felt as though I should look for other work though, and spent some time googling job vacancies on the Indeed website and looking at other branches of Reynolds & Rhodes, wondering if I would be able to get a transfer if I needed to.

Feeling somewhat lighter hearted at my decision to speak to Max, but still shaky from my recent trip back and the shock of Gregory not being there when I needed him, I poured myself a glass of wine and, taking a sip, went upstairs to prepare myself for bed.

In my bedroom I gazed from between the curtains at the back garden, which seemed to stretch into infinity in the darkness. The pond gleamed in the dusk, and I could hear faint splashing sounds as goldfish curved through the water. The occasional flutter and hoot could be heard from the inky sky as owls scoured the garden and the allotments for tasty mice.

Stars twinkled in the blackness and, gazing up at them, I wondered if Ursula was up there, and Margaret and baby Henry, all of them swinging from the stars, taking a well earned rest after living such traumatic lives. I took another sip of wine when, to my shock, a fanfare echoed throughout the still air. Shaking my head, thinking I must be hearing things, and knowing that I certainly hadn't had enough wine to be drunk, I pulled back slightly from the window. But my eye was caught by something strange, something so strange that I moved nearer again because I couldn't believe what I was seeing.

The fanfare rang out again, and a great army of men came into view, unkempt bloodthirsty men that marched over the allotments, annihilating all our carefully planted vegetables. Their big heavy boots tramped over the lawns and the flower beds, flattening all the beautiful flowers and churning the borders into sticky slimy mud.

The noise was so loud, a terrible din of marching boots and raucous voices, neighing horses and pounding hoof beats, that at first I worried what the neighbors would think. But coming to my senses, I realized that I wasn't in my bedroom at Mitchell Road any longer, that this house and garden didn't exist yet, and that all this colossal uproar was happening in another time and another place. King Henry's men didn't know that they were ruining my garden and my allotment, but in their time were marching across the drawbridge and into the grounds of Warblington Manor.

The royal standards fluttered ahead in a chilly breeze, and a black carriage, jolting and jerking, the king's arms emblazoned on the side, brought up the rear. A bedraggled looking lackey, a young boy not much older than young Henry Stafford, walked alongside, struggling to pull its thin wheels out of the thick mud. I could hear a harsh voice shouting at him from within. It wasn't night time any more, but day, and it was cold. The sky was grey dotted, with black angry looking clouds that spat rain as if from a great gaping mouth.

Looking down at myself, I saw that I wore my mourning

gown again, and not the jeans and T-shirt that I had dressed in that morning. When I turned from the window I realized that I was in my bedchamber and a fire burned in the grate, belching out smoke so grey and noxious that an unbearable tickle in my throat made me cough. I knew with a sinking heart that this was King Henry's retinue, and that he had come to claim Warblington Manor — had come to turn me from my childhood home, to banish me and my husband, Henry Stafford, and my great brood of children, back to the hustle and bustle of London and to the home of Henry's family. My heart ached at the thought of leaving, for I felt closer to my mother here than anywhere else in the world.

I ran downstairs and to the great heavy front door and, flinging it open, went into the garden pursued by my husband, Henry, his skinny legs moving in a blur, faster than I'd ever seen before. He glared at me, his bulbous eyes bulging from his high domed forehead. "Ah, this is it then, Ursula." He pointed at the house with a long skinny finger. "Warblington Manor will be your home no more."

Our attention was diverted by the royal carriage coming to an abrupt halt in front of us, its two gleaming black horses neighing and prancing. The army of men marched forward and began to enter the house, taking off their swords and flinging them with almighty clashes into an untidy heap on the tiled entrance way floor. The window of the carriage rattled down and King Henry peered out, showing his face which, since the last time I'd seen him, was as pink and puffy as a bloated pig's bladder.

As befitted the king I curtseyed deeply, alongside Henry Stafford, who bowed his head so low, his bulbous forehead almost touched his knees. Inside the carriage I saw that one of King Henry's legs rested on the seat opposite to him, and I noticed that a bloody bandage covered a suppurating wound on his thigh which stank worse than the muddy beaches at Langstone Shore. I took several deep breaths of the fresh salty air to fortify myself.

"Ah, Ursula, my belle Ursula. I wish to reside here this evening. Have you food and ale aplenty?"

"Oh yes, sire, food and ale enough for many men."

His multitude of chins wobbled with glee and, clapping his thick hands together to alert his man servant, he made to get out of the carriage. As if from nowhere his retinue gathered around him like seagulls spying a dead fish. As he alighted from the carriage, he fixed me with a penetrating gaze, the clear blue eyes of his younger handsomer self now rheumy grey slits.

I gazed back, my face a mask, not showing the turmoil that was inside, not showing the grief at the murder of my mother. King Henry stated, "Two days, Ursula Pole. You have two days to pack your possessions and take your husband...." Here he eyed a genuflecting Henry Stafford with disdain, "And your children back to London. This is at the order of the king."

Leaning heavily on his man servant, he walked slowly into Warblington Manor, without once looking back. And then my eyesight began to waver and King Henry's retreating back began to blur, the splendid colors of his clothes becoming muted. I awoke still standing at the window in Mitchell Road, gripping the windowsill while looking out at the garden. I felt dizzy and sick, and more so than ever because of the strong smell of fruit emanating from the half-drank glass of wine at my side.

Lying on my bed, worrying now about having to pack so quickly for the trip to London and the grim look on King

Henry's overfed face when he had given me such a strict order, I took several deep breaths and, trying to put such problems from my mind, closed my eyes and willed myself to sleep.

Chapter Fifteen

I awoke early and gazed around, conscious of the fact that I was Hannah Palmer, who lived on Mitchell Road in Bedhampton, Havant, in Hampshire, and as we used to say in school, England, the Universe. I was not Ursula Pole, who had been given orders by King Henry the Eighth of England to up sticks and leave her home in Warblington Manor within the next two days.

My heart pounding, I realized that I was safe and would not be homeless any time soon. I was so afraid of the awesome task of packing all my family's possessions in such a short space of time. Luckily for her, though, Ursula would have had her ladies to help, as well as her eldest daughter, Dorothy. I didn't think there was any way at all that she could rely on Henry Stafford to pack anything at all, let alone a crate full of his own belongings, and to sort out his many fancies and fripperies.

Arriving at work I saw that Sarah was already there, so I peeked around her office door to say a quick hello and then go into the kitchen to put the kettle on. I looked from the window at the pots of flowers basking in the early morning sunshine, their sweet faces turned up to the sun's yellow rays. The sky, a hard pale blue, arched overhead. Sipping my coffee, I went to Max's office to check his diary. Puzzled, I saw that he had crossed through today, and the words Annual Leave were written on the page with a thick black pen.

Shrugging and wondering why he hadn't said anything to me about a day off, as he usually did, I returned to my office and tried to get on with some work. I had plenty to do, as Max had left several tottering piles of files for me with instructions for letters to be typed, phone calls to be made, and appointments to be put in the diary. As well as, of course, the inevitable filing.

Thinking about it, though, I was a bit put out that Max wasn't there. I'd prepared myself mentally to have a word with him about Gregory Walsh. Not only to tell him that I finally believed him about his past life experiences as Gregory, but to get a first-hand account of what had actually happened to him when he'd disappeared from Ursula's life. I wanted to know if he'd realized how badly hurt she was by the whole situation.

As well as that, I didn't really like having to actually say sorry for not believing the "I'm so Great" Max Reynolds in the first place. He'd love the fact that I was bowing down to him, I was sure of that. What an irritating man he could be at times. Trying not to think about Max and the whole sorry situation, I worked on steadily for the rest of the day, with just an interruption from Stuart at one point about a problem with somebody's will, and a chat with Sarah in the kitchen when I made yet another cup of coffee.

What on earth would I do without coffee to get me through the day? Glancing at my Fitbit with such a disappointing number of steps — barely three thousand — I decided then and there that I should stop the coffee and start drinking water all the time. That way surely I would lose weight without worrying about how many steps I'd done. *Hmm, I suppose I could give it a try.*

Finally five o'clock came around, and I went outside to the parking lot and got into Daphne, my little red Mini. Havant seemed busier than usual, with plenty of people going in and out of the shops along the High Street. Perhaps because it was such a lovely sunny day, and even now at this time the sun shone from a blue sky with just a few cobwebby clouds floating about like shredded cotton wool balls.

I had an urge to go to Warblington again to the ruin, but I really wasn't sure if I was up for another trip back just yet. I still felt pretty upset about the last time, and the fear that I always felt in the presence of King Henry just never seemed to go away. I decided that I didn't want to bump into him any time soon, so would probably give the ruin of Warblington Manor a miss tonight.

Deciding then that I'd go straight home, I'd just driven past the Bear Public House and what I thought was the now derelict Streets, the ironmongers, when I noticed that the building was no longer empty, but had been turned into what looked like a trendy cafe bar, similar to Mooch on Cosham High Street. I felt a momentary pang at my Nan's favorite store not being open for hardware any more, but realized that it was better than the building going to rack and ruin. I glanced in as I cruised slowly by, and could see that Havanti Coffee House, as it was called, was fairly busy, with quite a few tables occupied.

Up ahead the traffic lights turned to red, and I found myself directly outside the cafe bar with a really good view inside, particularly of people sitting at tables in the window. Suddenly, with a sinking heart, I saw that one of those people was Max, my boss Max Reynolds, sipping elegantly at his no doubt latte coffee, and leaning forward talking animatedly to a woman who sat directly opposite him. A woman who, at first glance I mistook for my sister, Claire. But glancing again, I realized that it wasn't her, but somebody who looked so much like her, from her blonde hair and tanned skin to her micro miniskirt and low cut top, that they could have been twins. *Oh my God*, I thought with a totally irrational feeling of jealousy. That little green imp that liked to sit on my shoulder and whisper nonsense in my ear was back. Max had found himself another Barbie.

~*~

"Your mother is an interfering wench," stated Henry Stafford as he paced our bedchamber, back and forth, back and forth, his skinny legs as rounded as if he had been riding a horse, or perhaps had rickets when young. "Her prophecies, her spells and potions — is she a witch, Ursula? Is your mother a witch?" He leaned close, his neck stretched and taut and his nose almost touching mine. "Should King Henry learn of this abomination?"

I kept quiet as I sat on the edge of our bed, for this was our first bedchamber together as a married couple, our first bed and this — I rubbed the large mound of my belly — our first child. I had been so happy and excited at first, longing for a boy child, as Henry did also. And while Henry wasn't the ideal husband, I was determined to make the best of it. But it seemed today as if Henry's ill temper had reached a breaking point.

I tried to think back, to understand what Henry was talking about. But as far as I knew, only a hazy conversation had taken place. "Hmm," I remembered my mother saying as my father looked on fondly and she ran her caring hands over my bump. "This could be the right shape and size for a boy child, but we shall have to wait and see."

"Well, Ursula." Henry came closer to me, crowding me. "You haven't answered my question. Should King Henry hear of this?"

A frisson of fear spread rapidly down my spine as I said, "Oh Henry, no, of course not. That was just guessing. My mother has no idea if the babe is a girl or a boy." A sudden memory of my mother dangling a pendant above my belly to see which way it turned came to my mind, and a hot flush suffused my body and my heart beat fast and hard.

"I've seen her give you potions, Ursula my dear."

"For sickness only, dear husband. The first months of child bearing can give a terrible sickness." A strong smell of fish from the beach seeped into the room, almost making me retch.

"It seems to me," stated Henry, as he straightened up and began pacing the room again, his soft shoes cutting swathes through the scented rushes and dust that lay upon the floor. "That you have an answer for everything, dear wife. Especially where your mother is concerned."

Before I could reply Henry swung around and, with the palm of his hand, slapped me across the face, rocking my head back so hard that it hit the wall behind. Stars as if from a night sky rocketed into my vision, and I gasped for air. Putting shaking hands to my face, I tried to stand up, but Henry pushed me back down onto the bed, his long fingers digging into my upper arms where I knew that, as well as on my face, telltale bruises would bloom later.

Proof, I thought to myself. *I would have proof.* But aloud I said, "No Henry, think of the child. Think of our baby, and please do not strike me again."

Henry, in a tiny, sneering voice, mimicked me as he carried on pacing. "No Henry, think of our baby, and please do not strike me again." He stopped suddenly and raised a clenched fist, and said in a conversational tone, "You are my wife, Ursula, my dear wife. My possession. You belong to me, and I shall strike you whenever the fancy takes me."

He came closer to me then, his fists ready, and I closed my eyes and, flinching, raised my hands to my face. Cowering on the bed, frightened for my life, I curled into a tight ball and promptly burst into tears that streamed like rain down my sore face.

There was a sudden pandemonium outside on the landing and the bedchamber door was flung open, admitting two of my brothers, Reginald and Arthur, who ran in and grabbed Henry between them by the upper arms.

"Unhand me, you fools," screeched Henry, kicking his legs in temper like a large black spider as my brothers carried him viciously from the room. "Unhand me."

Henry and Geoffrey, who had been loitering outside, watching with satisfaction as Henry was manhandled out, rushed over to the bed where I still cried pitifully, curled up tightly like the fetus that I carried in my belly.

"He will not harm you again, dear sister," said Henry, as he sat on the bed and stroked my long hair which, because of Henry's attack, had come undone from its hood and rippled in waves down my back.

"Never fear, Little Bear," said Geoffrey, his arrogant mouth set in a thin angry line. "We will teach him a lesson that he will never forget."

They left me then, and when I awoke centuries later as Hannah Palmer, my face still shone wet with tears.

Chapter Sixteen

"Thanks for holding the fort yesterday," said Max. "I had a bit of a family crisis and needed to take urgent annual leave. Anything to report back? Any problems?" He looked smart as always, dressed in a dark suit with a faint silver stripe running through it. His cream shirt open at the neck showed a mat of chest hair — thank God no medallion, though — which as usual I studiously avoided looking at and concentrated instead at a point just to the left of his ear.

Huh, family crisis, I thought. *What, with a Barbie doll?* But I shook my head and said, "No, nothing. I just got on with the work that you left for me. I posted out all the letters and finally got all the filing done."

"Brilliant. Thanks, Hannah. Now then, have you time for dictation?"

I nodded as I sat down on my usual chair opposite him and prepared myself with notebook and pencil.

I wasn't feeling good today, not after the awful experience as Ursula in her supposedly happy newly wedded life with Henry Stafford. He had struck her so hard that I was still reeling from the shock. Some of the things that he'd said about my mother, Margaret Pole, were bothering me too. I mean, there was no way that she had been a witch. Ridiculous.

Gazing beyond Max's head out of the window, I saw that the rain from early this morning had stopped and the sun was valiantly trying to shine as it dodged amongst the clouds, some of which still looked a little black around the edges. A few cars cruised by on the old Havant Road, and a man walked past wearing a waterproof walking jacket and carrying a rucksack, that hung from his back like a child being given a piggy back.

"Are you okay, Hannah?" I looked up at Max, who actually did look genuinely concerned. A faint scent emanated from him, sort of citrusy and sweet, which I assumed was aftershave, as he looked a touch more clean shaven than usual.

Huh, I thought maliciously. *Probably for the benefit of his latest Barbie doll.*

"Not really," I replied. "I'm a bit tired. But in any case, I have an apology to give you."

"Really?" he said, beaming all over his face, and when I didn't reply straight away, he said, puzzled, "What for?"

I told him everything that Sarah had told me about Gregory Walsh. "So you see," I said, "I've no choice but to believe you now, have I?"

"Why? Because Sarah, also known as Elizabeth the First, Queen of England, told you that I am indeed Gregory Walsh, lowly gardener?" He chuckled then, which actually did make me smile, my first of the day. He leaned forward, his forearms on his desk. "Seriously, though, I told you it was the truth, Hannah. And I think I gave you definite proof of that too." He glanced down towards his chest, and I knew that he was referring to the little crescent moon scar that both he and Gregory had just below their left nipple.

"Yeah, okay then. So as you truly are Gregory, then tell

me why he's disappeared from Ursula's life. Where is he?"

"I'm not sure if I can tell you that, Hannah." He sat back in his chair and put both hands behind his head so that his shirt stretched tight against his chest, making my heart beat just that little bit faster. Why did he have to do that? "If it hasn't happened to you yet in that life, then...." He let the words hang in the air, unsure of what to say next.

"That's rubbish, Max. The truth of it is that you don't want me to know, do you?"

He frowned and looked unsure as he sat forward again. "It's not that. It's just not right to tell you things that happened in the past that you weren't part of. It's difficult to explain."

"Is he dead, Max? Is that what it is? You can tell me. I have to know some time."

"Of course he's dead — they all died," he said impatiently. "They lived centuries ago. Ursula is dead too."

"That's not what I mean, and you know it isn't. Has he been murdered, and has it got something to do with Henry Stafford?"

He said impatiently, but with a slightly worried look, "Good God, Hannah, what a question. Look, I know this is important, but can we meet after work and talk about it? I must get this dictation done today. It's pretty urgent now, and with not being here yesterday, I've got stuff to catch up on."

Before I could help myself I said sarcastically, "Oh, where do you want to meet, Max, Havanti Coffee House?"

Choosing to ignore the sarcasm and probably not really understanding it as yet, he replied, "Hey, that's a good idea. I went there yesterday — great place. Actually, I thought of you while I was there, because it's similar to the cafe bar we went to in Cosham — that place called Mooch. Do you remember, Hannah, the place where you walked out on me?" He grinned mischievously.

Ignoring the bit about walking out on him, and because other matters were at the forefront of my mind, I said, "Yes, I remember Mooch very well, Max. Actually, I saw you in the new cafe bar yesterday. You were sitting at a table in the window."

"Yes, I was. You should have come in, I would have introduced you —"

"Oh yes, Max." I began to stand up, forgetting all about the dictation that he so urgently wanted me to take and, almost throwing my notebook and pencil onto his desk in frustration, said, "What would you have done? Introduced me to your latest Barbie doll?"

For a split second Max looked blank, but a slow dawning realization began to come over his face and he started to laugh, proper real laughter that brought tears to his eyes so that he had to wipe them away with his knuckles.

"I don't know why you're laughing," I said, totally riled up now and prepared for a fight.

"Oh Hannah, honestly. Yeah, I know what you mean. She looks similar to your sister, I suppose. All that long blonde hair and tanned skin. I noticed that she got a lot of longing looks from some of the male customers — because of the short skirt, I suppose — but —"

"Yeah, like all of the women that you ever hook up with." I stated sullenly.

"Well, okay then, Hannah, break the mold," he said, standing up and putting his palms down on the desk with a slap. "You don't look like a Barbie doll, so why don't you go out with me?"

"You must be joking," I said between clenched teeth, my arms straight at my sides and fists balled. "I wouldn't go out with you in a month of Sundays." Now where had that expression come from? Preparing to leave the room now, I turned towards him and said with venom, "Anyway, Ken, how can I go out with you now that you've got a new Barbie?"

Holding my head high, I stalked across the room feeling quite pleased with my parting shot, when Max said, with just a hint of laughter in his voice, "Well, actually, Hannah, the Barbie that you saw me with in Havanti Coffee House is none other than my sister, Alison. So there."

I even heard a childish, "Na na na na na," followed by a lot of laughter as I made my way back to my office.

~*~

I went home that evening feeling very downhearted, and spent my time applying for jobs, not only as a legal secretary but also as a shop assistant at a bakery in Purbrook called Betty's Baps. If my own sister could have a career change for a while, then why couldn't I? I also sent a couple of emails, one to Reynolds & Rhodes in Denmead and the other to the branch in Waterlooville, asking if they had any vacancies for a transfer at the moment.

God knew what Max would say to that, but I really thought that the time had come for us to stop working together. The bricks were finally down, and it seemed at the moment that there was no going back. His sister? Oh my God, did he really expect me to believe that? Unfortunately, he was putting me in mind of a rather large spider sitting in a web spinning tales. And if Max was determined to spend his life as a Ken to his Barbie, then so be it. I had a gut feeling that it was time I backed out of his life for good.

Restlessly I stood up and, switching off my laptop and putting it neatly on the coffee table, peered from the window. The evening had brightened up considerably, and the black edged clouds that had blocked the warmth of the sun earlier had melted away like cotton candy on a tongue, leaving a perfect clear blue sky. I stretched my arms above my head and rolled my shoulders, thinking that perhaps a walk to the park would clear my head a little, as well as earning me just a few Fitbit steps.

People, out in their gardens now that the weather had improved, were busy tidying up, mowing the lawns, weeding the borders, and cutting back unruly plants, making me think of my lover Gregory Walsh. My heart beat that little bit faster at the thought of what might have happened to him, and to his father and sister.

I walked to the bottom of Mitchell Road, past the two story blocks of elderly people's retirement flats, and then through massive ornate gates and into Bedhampton Park, where I found a bench near to the playground and sat down, automatically turning my face up to the sun. I listened to the children as they played on the swings and the slide, aware of their high-pitched voices and screams as they spun on the merry-go-round until they were blurry as a rain washed window.

After a while the children's voices began to fade, and I felt a chill like a cold hand against my skin. Opening my eyes I was surprised to find that the sun had gone in behind a huge bank of golden tinged clouds, and that so very suddenly dusk had fallen.

Oh no, not now, I thought as I realized that I was no longer sitting in the sunshine in Bedhampton Park, but that I was in the pretty walled garden on the grounds of Warblington Manor. I wore a heavy black silk lined cloak over my gown, as the air felt chilly even though it was spring time, as daffodils and tulips shone bright yellow, red, and orange in the borders.

Gazing up, I saw that stars were beginning to twinkle in the sky, and as a sliver of moon showed its face, I felt a chill run down my spine.

Quickly I got up from where I'd been sitting on the stone bench, my only thought that I should be indoors by now. What on earth was I doing sitting in the walled garden in the near dark? Anybody could be abroad at this hour. Hastily, treading softly, my cloak pulled tightly around me, the hood over my head, I made my way through the shadowy garden, when all at once I saw a figure ahead of me. A figure I recognized immediately, if only by the skinny bowed legs, as my husband, Henry Stafford.

What was he doing creeping around outside at this time? Intrigued, I followed him deeper into the woods and along moon lit paths ankle deep in crispy leaves and muck. I crept behind him for what seemed a long time, as we had come far enough into the woods to arrive at Gregory's cottage, where I saw that smoke curled lazily from the chimney. I watched as Henry peered through the tiny windows and then, as he must have seen somebody there, backed away quickly and went to stand in the shadows beneath the overhanging branches of the trees.

The cottage door opened suddenly and Gregory stood on the door step in a sliver of candlelight that lit up the tiny back garden. I could see the small wooden pens that he had made with his own hands, and hear chickens clucking and fussing.

"Who is there?" asked Gregory into the blackness. "If there is anybody there, then show yourself." He walked away from the cottage and through his garden, closer still to the black shape of Henry, who stood hidden in the shadows. I was near enough to touch Gregory as he passed by, but I didn't, for I had a feeling that I couldn't be seen and that I was just a bystander, as I had been with my mother, Margaret Pole, on the day of her execution.

"I know you are there, Henry Stafford," said Gregory quietly. "Show yourself so that we may talk and our differences be reconciled. Look...." He turned a full circle, his arms open wide. "I am unarmed and not dangerous."

He was no more than an arm's length from the dark shape of Henry now. There was a long silence, heavy with anticipation, and in a split second, less than a blink of an eye, I saw a flash of silver. Then I heard a heartfelt groan as Gregory's white shirt blossomed red as the roses he tended so carefully in the gardens of Warblington Manor.

I stifled a scream, my hands covering my mouth as he sank to his knees on the hard ground. He held on to the knife with both hands as, desperately, he tried to wrench it from his chest. But it was too late for, with an anguished sob, he collapsed full length amidst the dust and the dirt. The dark shape that was Henry Stafford melted away into the blackness as if he'd never been there at all.

The very essence of Gregory Walsh was fading rapidly as I knelt beside him and clasped his limp hands in mine. They were cool, and not warm and vibrant as they were the last time we had met. I gazed at his lovely face, at his beautiful full lips that I'd so loved to kiss, and at his eyes that, when we made love, became a muted hazy green.

His breathing was rapid now and he was panting, taking short sharp breaths.

There was a precious split second of recognition as his lips curled into a smile, and he said, "Ursula, my Little Bear, you came." And then, with one last sigh, he was still, so very still, and I knew he was gone.

Chapter Seventeen

I awoke in my bedroom at Mitchell Road with sunlight streaming through the thin curtains, throwing myriads of sparkle onto the cream painted walls and laying in golden pools on the carpet. Sarah was sitting on the edge of the bed, holding tightly to both my hands. The salty taste of tears lay on my tongue and coated my teeth like a furry plaque. I felt tired and lackluster, and my head ached.

"Hey, here, Hannah, take these."

Sarah handed me two tablets, and without even asking what they were I swallowed them down with the water that she'd given me. Plumping up the pillows, she helped me to lie back against them as if I were an invalid or somebody old and frail.

"Oh, Sarah," I said, as memories came crashing into my mind. "Gregory is dead."

"Hey, I know," she soothed. "I know, Hannah. But you have Max. Max is Gregory, Gregory is Max. Do you understand?"

I put my hands to my face in despair and, shaking my head, said, "No, they are not the same people, Sarah. Gregory was a good man, not like Max. He's only interested in Barbie dolls."

Sarah looked faintly put out. "Hey, I'm sure there's more to Max than that, Hannah."

"There isn't, Sarah. He ridicules me, and I saw him in that new cafe bar in Havant with another Barbie doll, who he tried to pass of as his sister."

"Hey, well, it probably was his sister. I know he has one — she's called Alison. Why would he lie?"

"What? A sister who looks just like my sister? Like a Barbie? He must think I was born yesterday." Sarah shook her head in frustration and opened her mouth to speak, when another memory came to me and I said, "Henry Stafford murdered him."

Sarah stood up and began pacing up and down the room. "Hey, I always suspected that. Was it poison or a knife?"

"A knife," I told her quietly. "And in cold blood. Gregory showed him that he was unarmed, and asked if they could talk to reconcile their differences. There was no fight, no self-defense."

Sarah shook her head regretfully. "Hey, there was no body found, you know, Hannah."

"No body?" I said, pulling myself upright against the pillows. "But he died just outside his cottage in the woods. Surely he must have been found by somebody."

"Hey, probably by his father and sister. They would almost certainly have buried him."

Puzzled, I said, "But surely if they'd been inside the cottage the night that Henry murdered Gregory, they would have come out to see what was going on. They would have heard something."

"Hey, you would have thought so," she replied. "Maybe they weren't there then but came home the following day and then found the body. We'll never know, Hannah."

Thoughts whirled around my head, senseless stupid thoughts that I would never have an answer to, but then the worse thing of all occurred to me. "Oh Sarah, Gregory died because of me. If he hadn't been having an affair with me...." I let the words go. I couldn't bear to say any more.

"Hey Hannah, Henry Stafford was an evil man. You mustn't blame yourself."

I nodded and, feeling even more worn out and tired, laid my head back down amongst the soft pillows.

Sarah smiled and said, "Hey, get some more sleep, Hannah. I'm going to work, so I'll tell Max you're not feeling good."

"Work." I'd forgotten all about work. Why couldn't it be the weekend? "Oh God, Max is really busy at the moment. He needs me." I flung back the covers and attempted to get out of bed, but Sarah pushed me down and hustled me back into bed, tucking me in and fussing around as if she was my mother.

"Hey no, Hannah, you're in no fit state. I'll help Max out. Luckily, Stuart is at the Denmead office today, so I'm relatively free. Don't worry. Get some sleep."

Giving in entirely, I said, "Thank you, Sarah, I owe you one."

Giving the duvet one last pull into place, she left the room with a wiggly wave of her fingers, and I snuggled down deeper into the warmth of the covers and closed my eyes.

I awoke later, much later, to see that it was getting light, the sun rising in a vibrant red hue on the horizon. I gazed around, alarmed and disorientated, because I was not in my bedroom at Mitchell Road, nor in the bedchamber at Warblington Manor. But I knew for sure that I was Ursula

Pole, so where was I?

From the bedchamber window I saw trees wearing the vibrant leaves of autumn, and could hear the faint rumble of carriage wheels from the busy turnpike. Then it came to me that of course, I was in London at Henry Stafford's family home, where I was banished to after King Henry took Warblington Manor away from me. I gazed at my hands that for some strange reason were picking and plucking at the bedsheets, and with an awful sinking feeling I saw that they were old and wrinkled, and that I was barely a mound beneath the silk counterpane.

I closed my eyes, willing myself to be back in Mitchell Road as Hannah Palmer, and not here in a bedchamber, centuries in the past. For I knew now with a startling clarity that this would be the final time, my final time going back. For today Ursula Pole was dying.

~*~

It was only August, yet already the leaves on the trees were turning their colors and transforming magically from somber green to vibrant shades of magenta, gold, and scarlet, and even a type of blue and brown. When they were lit by the glow of the sun they were indeed one of the most beautiful sights to be seen. I watched them flutter as if touched by invisible fingers and etched as if they were a painting against the harsh blue of the summer sky.

I was thin and old, and created barely a mound beneath the sheets that were tucked tightly around me as I lay there on my bed—my death bed. I picked and plucked at the bedsheets with my fingers over and over again—the reason why I did not know, but I could not stop. *Greensleeves* played somewhere nearby, and I longed to play that tune again, running my fingers quickly, deftly over the strings of my harp. But my hands were useless now, and gnarled as if they were old twisted tree roots.

The door opened with a creak and my daughter Dorothy came in, a grown woman now with children of her own. She had the great honor of being mistress of the robes to Queen Elizabeth the First. She had made me proud. She was a good girl, my best girl, closest to my heart. She ran gentle fingers over my forehead and, leaning over, kissed my brow, a kiss so light that it felt like the touch of an angel. She brought the smell of sunshine and cut grass inside with her.

The arrogant face of King Henry loomed into my vision, and I thought of the day that he had turned me out of Warblington Manor so many years before. I felt again the harsh punches from Henry Stafford's fists, and the overwhelming grief that broke my heart when my baby Henry died. I saw my mother, Margaret Pole, with her head on the block, and the axe glinting as it arced through the spring air.

I plucked faster and harder at the bedsheets, and noticed now that my breathing had become harsh and guttural. I did not like how it sounded, but I could not make it otherwise. My vision was disappearing, becoming cloudy, and the walls of my bedroom were wavering like the rippling sea at Langstone Shore. Oh, I wished I could go to Warblington Manor and walk the little lane to the old church of St. Thomas à Becket, and feel the sun warm upon my face.

"I think her time is near," I heard Dorothy whisper. Black clad servants scurried into the room and began covering the windows with dark hangings, so that the spectacular view of the garden and the sky and the vibrant leaves that would disappear from the trees when I was gone could not be seen.

The servants covered the mirror that hung over the fireplace with a black cloth, the very thing that I remembered doing with a joyous heart on the day that my husband, Henry Stafford, died. What a day that had been, a good day to be sure, for the murder of Gregory Walsh had been a terrible secret that I had kept for so many years. I felt Gregory's presence all around me today, and I wondered if he knew that soon we would be together again.

My children were gathering around the bed now, and as I opened my eyes for one last time I saw them all so clearly, each face held safe within me wherever I may go. Dorothy placed our old worn Bible tenderly in my hands, hands that had now ceased their picking and plucking at the bedsheets, and I felt comforted by her voice as she murmured from her own book, "Be strong and courageous, do not be discouraged, do not be afraid...."

I raised my eyes towards the sky and took one last deep breath, and in a heartbeat Ursula Pole was no more.

~*~

The sleek black car, purring like the sleek black cat that had curled on the hearth in Gregory Walsh's cottage, pulled up outside St. Thomas à Becket Church and sat waiting in a pool of afternoon sunshine. It was July and a fine day, the sun hot and hazy amidst white fluffy clouds that matched my beautiful white dress, which cascaded over me and Dad and the long leather back seat like a glass of foaming milk. The driver, wearing a smart dark suit and peaked cap, sat quietly in the front seat, his hands, clad in black leather gloves, idly smoothing the steering wheel.

I gazed from the car window at the church and the graveyard, where I knew that beneath a heart shaped stone, Eliza Walsh, Gregory's mother, lay, and my heart ached at Gregory's awful sudden death, and Ursula's too, and hoped that now they would be together forever. My eye was drawn to the cemetery's old yew tree, and the overhanging branches that sprouted from the massive trunk and overshadowed all the old leaning tombstones, turning them black as the rotting teeth of Mrs. Dawes, the midwife.

With a rumble, another sleek black car pulled up behind, and my three bridesmaids—Claire, Laura, and Alison—clad in sumptuous sky blue gowns, unfurled from the back seat in a froth of lace. Dad, peering over his shoulder, cut into my thoughts. "Good God, Hannah, I didn't think you'd really ask that Laura to be one of your bridesmaids."

"She's Claire's partner, Dad," I said as I watched Claire hold Laura's arm, her hand pale as a ghost against Laura's dark skin. Then Alison, her hair as blonde as Claire's, joined them. All three of them made me think of the chocolate cookies that Claire used to sell in Smith & Vosper—white, milk, and triple chocolate.

The scent of Larkspur and Cornflowers wafted from their bouquets as they peered into the open window of the car and giggled at me, sitting there like a queen, resplendent in my wedding gown. A circle of wildflowers sat upon my hair that fell in waves, dark and shiny as a horse chestnut, to my shoulders. I was definitely no Barbie.

Mum didn't come over to the car, but gave a little wave and ducked into the church with Ryan, who looked like a grown up in his smart dark suit. "She's too choked up," Dad had told me earlier as we waited at my childhood home in Cosham for the car to take us to the church. "She's happy for you, but sad too. Plus...," he pointed out quite seriously, it seemed, "She doesn't want to cry and spoil her make-up."

Dad pulled back the sleeve of his suit jacket to check his watch, and said, "Hannah, do you want to go in yet?"

"No," I said. "I want to be fashionably late."

The smell of the sea hung in the air, and if I listened carefully I could hear its gentle shushing as it rolled onto the stony shore. More people were arriving now, including Stuart and Sarah, who, going quickly into the church, glanced around as if they were going to be told off for being so last minute. And as Stuart was the best man, he really needed to get a move on. Out of habit I checked my Fitbit, but remembered that I'd left it behind, sitting on the dressing table in the spare room at Mum and Dad's. Today of all days, though, I didn't give a jot if the Fitbit police came after me. I was having time off.

My thoughts wandered back to Mum, who was disappointed that she hadn't been able to find out any more about our family connection to Margaret Pole and Henry the Eighth. I told her that William Palmer, a musician at King Henry's court, had been the lover of Ursula Pole's husband, and maybe that was the only connection to find. A mincer of a man, I'd almost said out loud, thinking of Gregory's words. They hadn't all been gay, though, I thought wistfully. Certainly not Gregory. But I didn't tell Mum about that, because such precious memories were only mine to keep.

"Come on," said Dad, breaking into my thoughts. "It's time. All the guests seem to have gone in."

The ancient church clock slowly chimed the hour of three, and with my heart beating almost into my throat, I uncurled slowly from the car, putting out my hand to Dad, who pulled me close as I stepped out onto the pavement. "My beautiful daughter, Hannah," he whispered into my ear. When I looked into his eyes, I would swear that there were tears hanging on for dear life to the very edge of his lashes.

My dress swung around me as I walked, my shaking hands holding tightly to Dad's arm. My three beautiful bridesmaids followed behind like a mini retinue — like a watered down version of King Henry and his men — into the tiny nave of the church, where just for a moment I stopped and stood still and, gazing down the aisle, saw my handsome future husband waiting for me.

Chapter Eighteen

King Henry dined sumptuously at Warblington Manor that day, the day that he arrived unannounced and turned the whole household into a turmoil and availed himself of my mother, Margaret Pole's, stores, which were then sadly depleted for many months after. He ate the plump roast breast of a swan, the head of a pig, its gaping mouth stuffed with a rosy apple, and a partridge's skinny legs, the bones of which he threw to my father's two dogs, Gilbert and Sturdy, as they lay growling and snapping beneath the table that groaned with the weight of the food.

He ate milk puddings and custard tarts, and downed ale aplenty and red wine by the barrel. If he carried on eating and drinking in that way, he would surely gain three chins and a belly as large as the city of London. Could that remark be construed as treason? God help me if it could. I thought my mother, Margaret Pole, was relieved when, in the dusky evening, the royal coach, followed by King Henry's vast retinue, ambled its way slowly across the opened drawbridge and onwards to London.

Restlessly I paced my bedchamber, where I had been sent as soon as King Henry showed his back. "You are weary,

168

Little Bear," my mother had said. "You must retire to your bedchamber." I leaned from the open window and breathed in the still night air. The scent of cut grass and flowers and dry earth slid into my nostrils and into my body, where my young veins still fizzed with the excitement of the king's visit. I wasn't weary—I didn't need to sleep. I wanted to see Gregory.

Thinking of our time together that afternoon, which had been cut short by such an unexpected visit, I sprang into action. Wrapping a cloak around my body and pulling the hood over my dark hair, I left the room and pattered silently, like a little mouse, down the stairs. Faint voices and laughter could still be heard from the kitchen quarters, where servants were still clearing away after the magnificent banquet that afternoon. Very quietly, with barely a screech on its rusty old hinges, I opened the huge back door and went out into the cool night air.

The woods, as I fled through them, stumbling on tiny stones and bits of dirt, were dark and creepy, the trees arching above me, their branches black against the darkening sky. Owls, their eyes shining like monstrous globes in the gloom, hooted overhead, making me jump while tiny animals and insects scurried amongst dry leaves on the mucky ground.

I saw Gregory straight away. He was in his garden, crouching down, settling the chickens, making soft clucking sounds as they strutted around picking and pecking at the earth. I threw back my hood with a flourish, showing him my face.

"Ursula," he said with surprise. "What brings you here at this hour?"

"We are to wed," I told him imperiously. "Bring your cat as a witness."

He threw back his head and laughed so hard the sound echoed around the woods, causing the birds to flitter and flutter from the trees in a panic. I then watched curiously as he plucked a blade of grass and, fashioning it into a circle, placed it on my finger as we stood together with the black cat Thomas at our side and, beneath the bright white light of the moon, said our wedding vows.

~*~

The office was quiet, as everybody had gone home. Well, I wasn't sure if Max was still in his office—I hadn't dared go back in since my outburst earlier about his sister. What must he think of me now? I was sure that he would be glad if I did get a transfer to another branch of Reynolds & Rhodes, or got a new job somewhere else. He was probably sick to the back teeth of my uncalled for jealous behavior.

I gazed from the tiny mullioned window at the sky, which at the moment looked harsh, angry, the blue almost obliterated by thick black clouds that looked ready to burst. I definitely needed to get to my car before it started to rain. A strong wind had picked up, and the bright flowers in the pots outside dipped and danced as if at a disco. Desultorily, I switched off my computer and, sighing, shrugged on my jacket. Picking up my bag, I prepared to leave for the day.

"I always preferred Sindy dolls, you know. I don't think I ever was a Barbie man. Not really."

I spun around to see my boss, Max Reynolds, standing framed in the doorway like a painting, entitled maybe, "Unknown Handsome Man." He'd taken off his suit jacket, so wore the black trousers with a belt that hung low on his hips, and a white shirt tucked in that was stretched tightly over his chest. His top buttons were undone as usual, showing a slice of hairy chest which, as usual, I studiously tried to ignore.

He began to walk slowly towards me, saying, "Sindy dolls have dark hair, not blonde. Lovely, shiny dark hair and a really sweet smile — and dark eyes too, not blue like a Barbie doll. I much prefer dark hair and dark eyes, Hannah."

He was close to me now, very close, and very slowly he put a finger to my chin and, tilting my face to meet his, said softly, his breath hissing in my ear, making me hunch my shoulders, "Do you remember climbing the steep stone steps into the bedchamber in the eaves, and listening to the twitter of the birds as we made love on that lovely soft bed?"

I opened my mouth to speak, to say perhaps, "No, Max, that was Ursula and Gregory, not Max and Hannah." But he silenced me with a finger to my lips and carried on speaking.

"Do you remember the scent from the rushes on the bedchamber floor, and the patter of the rain on the thatched roof as we lay together skin to skin and mouth to mouth?"

"Max, I—"

"Come to that Hannah…." This time he stared straight into my eyes. "Do you remember that hot sweaty night club, and all the words to 'You to me Are Everything?' and how good we felt in each other's arms as we danced?" I gazed at him in wonder, hardly believing what I was hearing, and started to speak, but he shushed me again and pulled me into his arms, where I fit so well into his body, my head just slotting in under his chin, like the missing piece of a jigsaw puzzle. He murmured into my hair, "There's only ever been you, Hannah, and I can't hold it in any longer. I have to tell you—I love you. I love you." Here he drew back and looked into my eyes. "Will you marry me?"

I shook my head slowly. "Boss and personal assistant. It won't work, Max."

"Well, you are thinking of a transfer to another branch,

aren't you? I got the email today."

I shook my head and smiled wryly as Max, to my utmost surprise, fumbled in his pocket and pulled out a ring fashioned from a blade of grass and pushed it onto my finger. Where on earth had he got that from? I was just about to ask but decided not to. Some things were better left unsaid.

"Well?"

I thought for a split second. "Oh — go on, then," I replied.

~*~

The wedding march sounded loudly in the confines of the small church, beautiful clear notes from the organ, as I began slowly, putting one silver slippered foot in front of the other, to walk down the aisle. I didn't know why, but gruesome images flashed through my mind. My mother, Margaret Pole, whom I'd mourned for so long, her poor vulnerable neck waiting on the block; and Henry Stafford, his face contorted with rage as he hit my face with a resounding slap; and then, the malicious look on the face of King Henry as he banished me from Warblington Manor.

Ryan gave me a cheeky grin and a thumbs up sign as, smiling and floating past as if in a dream, my feet barely touching the ground, I glanced at Mum, who was sniffing and holding a tissue to her tear stained face. Candles guttered fitfully from the deep window embrasures and shone blindingly bright on the altar as, with a gentle squeeze, Dad let go of my arm. I stepped forward to join him, my groom that "Unknown Handsome Man."

We stood outside afterwards in the hot summer sunshine, the two of us, Mr. and Mrs. at last, our arms linked together like a chain — an unbreakable chain going back centuries, it seemed. I gazed towards the little heart shaped stone in the corner of the cemetery and thought of Gregory's mother,

Eliza, gone far too soon. And then, of course, of Gregory and Ursula, holding hands and kneeling amongst the chickens as they pledged their undying love for one another.

My brand new husband turned to me and, gently stroking my face, said, "Are you as happy as I am, darling? Ursula, my Little Bear."

I nodded as, gazing up into the unmistakable green gaze of Gregory Walsh, a not unpleasant shiver ran down my spine.

THE END

About the Author

Debbie Chase (married name Debbie Spink) was born in Emsworth in Hampshire in 1959, although she has lived in West Yorkshire since 1979. She is the eldest of five children (two sisters and two brothers) and has many nieces and nephews, great nieces and nephews, aunties, uncles and cousins, having come from a very large family. She has been married since 1984 and has one daughter, Lara and two cats Ruby and Teddy.

She has always been a reader and has enjoyed writing since school. Her proudest moment being when she achieved an A+ for an essay. She has had many short stories and poems for adults and children published in books and magazines. She has written four books, the first being part fact/part fiction and called "You to Me Are Everything." The second book based on a real life pet sitting job is called "The Confessions of a Pet Sitter (from the Pet's Point of View) and the third, the sequel to that book, "What A Catastrophe (Teddy's Tale). The fourth book is a book of poems. All four books are available to buy on Amazon as a paperback or kindle. She has also had two pocket novels ("Planning on Love" and "Romance on the Run") published with My Weekly magazine.

Her other hobbies are running, walking, swimming, yoga, pilates and Tai Chi. After many years of office work she is now partially retired and works part time in a baker's shop and is also an Examination Invigilator in a local school.

www.ingramcontent.com/pod-product-compliance
Lightning Source LLC
Chambersburg PA
CBHW020128180626
46810CB00004B/1459